1984

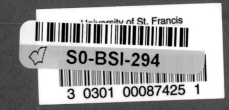
Michael A. Faletti
117 Seeser Street
Joliet, Illinois 60436

THE
SENSUALISTS

The Sensualists

by

BEN HECHT

JULIAN MESSNER, INC.

NEW YORK

Published by Julian Messner, Inc.
8 West 40 Street, New York 18

Published simultaneously in Canada
by The Copp Clark Publishing Co. Limited

Printed in the United States of America

Library of Congress Catalog Card No. 59-8834

To David O. Selznick
of Hollywood and the Moon

THE
SENSUALISTS

Mrs. Ann Lawrence faced herself in her bedroom wall mirror and studied her nudity with her husband's eyes. Or at least with the eyes he used to have when he loved only her, which she was reasonably certain was no more than six months ago.

Not an inch more, not a curve less, the mirror reported, snowy skin, reddish hair, fragile neck and pretty features meant for jesting, except the eyes—large, green and meant for looking innocent. A fine ensemble for thirty-two, including eight years of marriage. Ann thought, "Except for my breasts, I might still be a virgin."

She thought of her eight marriage years so full of her devotion that they were indistinguishable years. There were no landmarks of disillusions or disasters. Pictures went through her mind like the glossy advertisements in the magazines, the ones that advertised married couples in love with lawn mowers, cheese crackers, furnaces, bedsprings, floor mops, automobiles, beer foams and all the buyable Americana.

She had been the heroine of all those ads, the beaming wife in a rain of bargains. In addition to shopping sprees and always new packages to open, there had been bridge parties, vacation trips, theaters, books, home and restaurant dinners, Christmas holidays, gossip, golf, club dances. Not many dances. Henry looked on dancing as old fashioned. "It was invented by the Puritans as a sort of bunt that got you to first base, sexually. We boys don't have to bunt any more."

Remembering Henry's words had become painful. But she had to remember them. There were hardly any other words in her head. It was Henry's words that made the Lawrences different from the contented glossy couples in the advertisements. Henry was a sort of saboteur loose in American suburbia, where the chief excitements, according to Henry, are the collapse of your neighbor's marriage or the discovery that nymphomania has wrecked the Baptist choir.

And now the Lawrences would be the scandal canapé, the "Oh, by the way, have you heard" dessert. My God, how their friends would enjoy this splitting up. More than the usual marriage flop in their golfing, partying, garden club suburban area of glibness. Because nearly all of Henry's best friends in Englewood regarded him as a troublesome misfit. And her own friends, Elsie Hartnett excepted, had a similar secret hostility toward her. Toward her figure, chiefly. She looked again into the mirror. It was a figure that had outwitted marriage. She remembered Henry talking as they lay in the sun beside the club pool. Some youngish bathing-suited matrons were floundering in and out of the water.

"How can they be so immodest?" she asked Henry, as she noted bosoms, buttocks and bumptious pelvises half in the open. "They're not immodest," said Henry, "they're merely nude. They look just as respectable with their flesh uncovered as in their winter minks. More so, I swear. Respectability takes over where desirability ends." Ann asked, "Why should a bit of fat here and there make a woman undesirable?" "Because," Henry said, "at the moment only my eyes are involved. I can imagine plump thighs and a dropsical behind being no end alluring if they were kept out of sight until needed. Female flesh has very little to do with sex attraction. Men usually seduce character and hop into bed with personality. Occasionally they are stirred by some bit of fetishism—Mama's coiffure on a tart, etcetera."

What a fool she had been to imagine smugly that Henry's information was the product, like her own, of psychological brooding. The villain had been speaking out of experience. How much? How long? How could she ever look at him again, knowing now what he was, without spouting her outrage into their world? But she must. This was one scandal that would not delight the golf links and the club bar. "I love him," she thought, "horrible man, I love him. I'm going to hang onto him like mad."

Tears came, and she turned from the mirror. A weeping nude was too pathetic. Like a spotted evening gown. Useless. She put on her Chinese robe, Chinese slippers, and cursed the name of Liza King who had stolen her husband. That teeth-glistening, mascara-eyed, black-maned café singer leaped into her mind like a jack-in-the-box. She had been leaping thus for a week—since Ann had stood furtively in the café foyer and watched the bulbous-bosomed Liza sock out a song in the spotlight.

"I mustn't think of her," Ann thought. "I'll lose my temper and spoil everything." "Everything" was Ann's plan for the elimination of Liza King and the restoration of Henry Lawrence as a faithful husband, as only hers.

The jack-in-the-box figure of the husky-voiced chanteuse went out of sight and Ann brushed the "guitarlike curves" of her hair. That's what Henry had called them—up to a night ago. She remembered him whispering in a darkened theater a week ago, "Your damned hair keeps making love to me." His hand touched it amorously. A week ago! The night after she had seen Liza King, and Henry alone at a ringside table ogling her bestially.

How could a man she had known so well become someone she didn't know at all? Become two men, one a brutal stranger? But Henry wasn't two. He was one. And this one man was a lie inside and out. His tenderness, love words, sexual and sentimental devotions were all lies. There was nothing real or truthful in love. At least in married love. It was all pretense, like the small talk you made on the club veranda, at the cocktail party. But it couldn't be that. A man couldn't be that much different from a woman, totally without love memories and their crop of pain.

Ann sighed. There was something too complex in a husband's infidelity for a sane wife to understand. A virtuous wife who had dotingly imagined for eight years that sex was a special invention for the Lawrences. How could he!

She shuddered not at the query but at the answers her cynical, defamatory Henry might make to such a question, if she were ever stupid enough to ask it. She recalled, "The trouble with wives is they think they are married to wives— to slightly different images of their own virtues." Good God, that was a month ago. He had been talking about her, Ann! Telling her furtively but righteously that he was being unfaithful. But he had always talked like that. Had he always been unfaithful, then? No! This Liza King was the first one. Her instincts said so. Or was it her stupidity? No, she was certain. Miss fat-lipped King was number one. Before that, Henry had been only intellectually wanton, happy to share all his roguery and sin with her.

"Oh, the rotten fellow," she sighed and started down the stairs slowly. Henry would be just launched on his grapefruit. There was time—until he had done away with the two soft-boiled eggs. Besides, she mustn't let him see her trying to eat. He would see her unable to swallow a piece of toast and realize instantly that his infidelity was known. That's the kind of an unfair, rotten genius Henry was. But she'd show him! "By God," she thought, "I'm almost as full of lies as he is!"

Ann sat down in the hallway. She scowled at Henry's muffler hanging over the couch arm in the living room beyond. He had dropped it there at two-thirty this morning. She had watched from her bedroom door. He had come in softly, grinning in the dark like a horrid stranger, thrown down his muffler and gone to the phone. Hardly forty minutes from his strumpet's side and he must say good night to her again, hear her thief's voice again. "As he used to do when he was wooing me," Ann grimaced.

She addressed herself in the hallway, as a troop before battle. Casual. She must bring nothing into the open. She must take advantage of her single asset—that he was still intent on deceiving her. And, using this asset, maneuver him out of the country—and Liza King's voluptuous arms.

"How can he prefer her to me?" she thought. How could he go to another at all? A coarse nothing of a female who had nothing to offer—except sin. That was obviously her lure. She could add a new ingredient to sex by making Henry feel like an adventurous safeblower instead of a stale suburban husband.

Ann brooded in the hallway, allowing time for the soft-boiled eggs to enter Henry's stomach. What a bargain the inlaid frame mirror had been. She stared at it possessively, remembering its auction sale. "Going, Going, Gone." Like Henry now. Liza King would hang him up on her wall—temporarily. It was no place for Henry to hang. It would ruin him. Not only his publishing business, his fine home, but his soul.

Ann frowned with deeper thoughts. She would have to lure Henry away from sin. But how could a wife compete with sin? The wildest passion a wife had to offer only made her more a wife. Whereas a cool kiss from Miss King probably shook Henry to his roots with a sense of drama and sin. "And, of course," she thought, "sex is more important when a man uses it to make a woman love him instead of to keep a wife contented." As—before they were married—

14

she and Henry. But that was an entirely different situation. She tabled it like a wrong document and remembered Henry talking, "In sex the male is more a connoisseur than a participant. He judges the charm of a sexual bout by the transports he's able to inspire in his companion." Ann said at that time, "How wonderfully unselfish you are, darling." Henry answered, "Unselfishness doesn't figure. It's just that a man's capacity for vanity is greater than for sensation."

Perhaps, thought Ann now, that was the whole explanation of his infidelity. He had met up with a bedroom Calliope. But how had he known she was that when he was making his first coy overtures? And why was she thinking all this sex psychology? As if she were boning up to join some orgy. She had to think now, before facing him at breakfast, or she would erupt with telltale thoughts at the sight of his evil face. "And in bed," she continued, "there's the novelty. And contrast. Different skin, curves, texture, and different mechanisms at work. Different sounds, words, secrets. And stories. She has stories to tell him, of course. Of her sinful past, now ended in his Tristan arms . . . oh, God!

"But I couldn't stand it if a man were different from Henry," she scowled. "I'd freeze. Different skin, different hands. I couldn't possibly feel anything but disgust. With myself, of course. But not Henry. Good old sinful Henry." She remembered his face at the café table, with its drooling and dramatic grin for his singing strumpet. No disgust for Henry. "It's rotten unfair," she thought, angrily.

Then she thought, still angry, that her whole plan of

15

battle—the casual kidnaping to Bermuda—might be a silly mistake. Her best friend Elsie had won her husband back from the arms of his Vassar-graduated secretary by screaming at the top of her voice for two months, and threatening nightly to jump out of their bedroom window.

Ann shook her head. Sam Hartnett and Henry Lawrence were not of the same tribe of male. Sam was a moral bounder, who could be terrified out of extramarital pleasures by a little wifely hara-kiri. Henry was, intellectually, a brute.

Ann stood up and started for the breakfast nook. Young summer filled its windows with glowing light. Bird song and chatter were in the trees around the house. She was suddenly afraid to join the man sipping coffee and reading a newspaper. Her heart pounded and a match seemed to light itself in the pit of her stomach.

"I love him," she gasped inwardly. "Oh, God, I love him! I want him. I'll die if I lose him."

She stood, feeling her cheeks and throat whiten. It was impossible to be casual and cunning with these miserable sensations running through her. She would go back to her bed, pretend illness and postpone the kidnaping plot until tomorrow. But the gaunt, smoky-eyed face with its never-well-combed crest of black hair pulled her to the breakfast nook. Soiled though it was with the kisses of that Liza bitch, it was still the most alluring face in the world.

"I'm all right," she informed herself with a smile. Walking toward the table, she repeated, "No accusation. No

openings. I'm not supposed to know. Keep it all hidden—
keep him lying, and frightened."

"Good morning," she smiled.

Henry nodded. Hannah, their ancient servant, shuffled
in with the coffeepot. Ann looked at her dumpy, clown-
faced retainer and gathered strength from the familiar
wrinkles.

One of the things that distinguished the Lawrences was
that, unlike their neighbors, they never had maid trouble.
While other young suburban matrons suffered vociferously
over the disloyalty, thievery and stupidity of maids, cooks,
gardeners, etc., Ann had known none of these domestic
Waterloos in her eight years of wedlock. Hannah had come
into her life as Henry's bachelor caretaker, and adopted
his bride as a lovable fellow incompetent.

"Good morning, Hannah," said Ann.

The stubby, plump Hannah beamed. Her small face was
reddish and slightly whiskered.

"You lookin' like a bride today," Hannah chuckled. "Like
a young girl. Such fine eyes, always smiling. I love you,
modom." Hannah was a Croatian and somewhat archaic.
"She suspects something," Ann thought. "Or knows it. Of
course she knows. She knows Henry. And she thinks I'm a
fool and is sorry for me."

"Thank you, Hannah." The archaic one shuffled out. Hannah was the only housekeeper in Englewood who wore
slippers the day long.

"What's the matter?" Henry asked, from his newspaper.
She avoided the gray eyes but saw his face. That handsome,

17

thin face with its strong teeth hadn't changed in the years she had known it, except to grow stronger. But the mouth had been more smiling once.

"I asked what's the matter, dear."

"Guilty," she thought. "Guilty and frightened out of his wits." She must be very careful. The "dear" was always a signal of decks cleared for action.

"Nothing's the matter," Ann said. "How's the toast—too brown?"

"The toast is exactly right," he said, and paused, his eyes on her. She was looking away at nothing in particular. "Why the acting?" he added.

"What acting?"

"You come down with a chilly 'good morning' and flop into a chair and stare into space."

"I'm worried about the railroad strike, darling."

"You've managed to overlook our national problems in the past."

His eyes were still on her, obviously on the pulse beating in her neck. She turned her head and her long hair curtained the telltale throb.

"Is it because I came home late?" he asked.

"I've no idea what time you came home," she lied calmly. "I took a sleeping pill around eleven and passed out a few minutes after. What time *did* you get in?"

"Oh, sometime after that."

She smiled at his answer. He was too clever to take advantage of too neat an opening.

"What is it then?" he continued. "Are you ill?"

18

"I feel very well."

He smiled at her. "If you have something to say please say it. Don't sit there bristling like the fretful porcupine!" He mimicked her formal tone. " 'I feel very well.' Good God, you're a bad actress."

"I imagine there are better," she smiled, and held her breath. It was a slip. Liza King was a café performer. But they probably called themselves actresses.

"Aren't you going to eat?" he inquired. She tried the orange juice, and pondered her problem. How "act" before a man who knew every shading of your voice, to whose eyes your slightest change of expression was as revealing as a written confession? Whereas Henry, the unfaithful monster, could sit chatting across a table without a single inflection to betray him. It was practice, of course, that made him bland, blank and evil. But she had one advantage over him—his guilt. The sad advantage that wives had over erring husbands, their fear of being found out. However bland and blank Mr. Lawrence looked, this fear was in him. A fear of what? Of pain. Giving it as well as feeling it. She remembered Henry: "All husbands are criminals from every point of view but their own. And, usually, including their own." Good lord, he had been confessing to her for years. But it couldn't be. There was only Liza King.

He had not pursued the challenge of "better actresses," had not asked "who?" Her worst fear had been, since she had "found out," that he would want the thing brought into the open, that he was secretly eager to have the name Liza King explode between them.

19

But she knew again, as she watched him read and nibble his toast, that he wanted to keep on with his lies. Her hope deepened. His lies showed that he still wanted to deceive her, he was not ready to risk losing her.

Hannah came in with her eggs. Ann felt she could swallow them without betraying herself. She smiled at Hannah. Henry was staring at the drama page of his newspaper.

"I swear to God, I'm going to call off Dick Kiley's book. I'm not going to publish such a smug puritanical ass. The man's a throw-back. This is the goddamnedest boy scout dramatic review I've ever read."

"How odd," said Ann. "You've always admired him so."

"Darling, I never admired him," Henry answered. "A pontificating master of puerilities. I admired his wife Hazel. Hazel brought the book in. Hazel sat on the couch showing her legs. Early Chippendale. She sighed, wriggled her ample seat and finally stood over me, pushing one breast in my ear as I read the first two pages of the manuscript."

"Your original story was that you read five pages before you called off the seduction—by accepting the book," Ann smiled.

"One always forgets the details of a lie," he assured her.

"Oh," her voice jested, "*did* she seduce you?"

"I would never permit another man's wife to seduce me," he answered.

"Dear me, why such discrimination toward wives?"

"Perhaps because they're usually a little overweight," he smiled. "And besides, the wives of literary men are too accessible."

20

"You're a literary man."

"No, just a publisher." He returned to his newspaper.

She felt better. She could win, if she was careful. Of course, he had only to say, "Ann, I love someone else. I want a divorce," and she would lose. But, obviously, he was far from that speech. She must be careful not to drive him into making it.

But she wouldn't let him have his cake and eat it—like those wives who were willing to accept duplicity as proof that they were still safe. She wondered if Henry imagined she would be willing to allow him to preserve their home with lies instead of love.

She glanced at her villain of a husband, calmly reading, behaving as if he had not been in another woman's bed ten hours ago. And she instructed herself, "I mustn't be smug. Maybe he's only postponing telling me. Afraid of hurting me too suddenly. He's probably begged her for time—told her he couldn't poleax me without a little preparation."

She hoped the tightening of her lips and the impulse to bang him over the head with the coffeepot were not too obvious. Apparently they weren't. Henry started reading aloud a political speech by the President, and ridiculing it between paragraphs. He was working hard at something, Henry was.

"He's sorry for me," Ann thought, as he read, "and he can't bear to hurt me." She felt abruptly "aware" of him, as if she had never thought of him before. Nor had she. She had never thought of him as a stranger, as someone to be solved. He had, from the beginning, seemed entirely

"solved" in her mind. He was what she wanted him to be.
"Does any wife ever look beyond that?" she thought.

She was aware now of all the rest of Henry, posturing in
ominous shadow. She knew he was fearful of unmasking
himself in her eyes. It had something to do with "love."
But there were other considerations. However he might
pant in secret for Liza King, a major part of him was still
the husband-Henry. Her own charming and devoted Henry.
It would hurt him violently to give that fine fellow the
coup de grâce. To say to her, "The *me* you know is dead. I
hereby stab him in the heart and kill him." Telling the truth
would be a form of suicide.

Not only his pity for her, but for himself, were her assets.
"It won't be too hard to keep him," she thought. "I've
been exaggerating things. Magnifying them by my inexperi-
ence. After all, except for Henry, I'm still a virgin. Knowing
one man is a sort of virginity."

She could afford even a mite of tolerance and get around
to punishing him later. Poor Henry! To have to hurt someone you loved couldn't be much fun. And he did love her.

Telling cheap lies must make him cringe inside. She recalled a phrase Henry had admired in a book—"the agony
of villainy." That was two years ago. Before Liza. Then
how did he know the truth of the phrase? Because he'd always been a villain, always unfaithful? Ann breathed slowly.
That wasn't true. He had known its truth just as she had
recognized it. And she had never lied or cheated. One's imagination knew such things. No, Henry couldn't be having
too much fun with his Liza wench when every hour was

22

full of some sort of guilt or dread. Or was *that* fun, she thought. Did all the business of panic, guilt, dread add enticement to that coarse café yawler?

He finished his reading aloud.

"What's the matter with you?" he asked abruptly.

"Political speeches always bore me," she smiled, "although you read them very well."

"You're not bored," Henry said. "You didn't hear a word I read. And you keep changing color, from snow white to salmon pink." His voice became tender. "Please tell me what's upsetting you." He smiled and added, "Your hair looks remarkable in this light. As indecent and lovely as ever."

"I didn't want to tell you just yet." She looked boldly into his eyes and was startled by their wistfulness. His eyes were making love to her, or rather their years of life together were making love to her out of those familiar eyes. She wanted to weep and to hold him close. Perhaps that was what he wanted, to confess everything in her arms. If she could only be certain he didn't love the creature, didn't want to go gallivanting off with her permanently.

"I'm waiting," Henry said.

"Well," she smiled, "I've been planning a surprise for quite a while. Eight weeks in Bermuda. Just you and I. No chaperones. I wired the Marguery Hotel and made the reservation."

She brought her hand slowly to his and covered it.

"Now you know my dark secret," she said.

"You're being very arch." He looked at her.

"Forgive me," she smiled. "The prospect of a honeymoon naturally makes me a bit girlish. Darling, we don't have to stay the full eight weeks. If we don't like it and are not having a heavenly time, we'll come back. One groan from you and I start repacking. That's fair, isn't it?"

She thought, watching his careful smile, "He's thinking of his Liza. My God—he *is* in love with her! He's scared of losing her!"

"Couldn't be fairer," he said. "But what about Elsie and that big fishing spree in Maine? She's waiting for you."

"I loathe fishing," she answered, "and lumpy cabin cots are not ideal for honeymoons."

"Good lord, lechery this early in the morning," he grinned at her. "But I thought it was all settled about Maine. Sam and I were going to join you in two or three weeks."

She shook her coils of hair and thought, "Oh, what a rotten, unfaithful man. My lover. My husband. Afraid to lose his little café chippie." The top two buttons of her Chinese robe came undone.

"Well, well," Henry eyed the spectacle solemnly. "An interesting breakfast item."

She rebuttoned the robe.

"It's getting rather old," she said.

"Nonsense," he said, "lovely as ever."

"I was referring to the robe," she smiled.

"I'll be home early today," he said. She stared and thought, "Oh, what a bastard. Playing Pasha. With a harem." Her heart felt sickened with her own pretenses and the cool scoundrelism of this creature she still loved.

24

"Darling," she took his hand again, "please!"

"I'll be home at four."

"Please let's go to Bermuda. I need the change."

"I'll think about it," he said.

"No," she insisted. He finished his coffee. "Another cup?"

"No, Ann."

"Don't fool me," she said softly, "about Bermuda. Will you come?"

"I won't fool you," his voice was flat. "I've arranged my affairs to get away for a week or so—next month."

His affairs! The flatness of his voice, the stubborn look in his eyes filled in any missing vital statistics. He wouldn't go because he couldn't bear to part with Liza. He was afraid he'd lose her. It wasn't a sex fandango. It was a real love affair—a hussy with a hook in his heart.

Looking into Henry's face, Ann knew that the name Liza King was ready to explode between them. She had only to press righteously for her way and Henry, fearful of losing what he desired, would let her harry the truth out of him. He was averse, obviously, to giving up either of them. He obviously fought with Liza to keep his wife. Just as he was ready to do battle now to keep Liza.

She thought miserably, "He's crazy. That's worse than his infidelity—his craziness. Pretending to me there is no Liza King. And pretending to her that I don't mean anything to him, that our marriage is a stale, sexless relationship. That's why he can't go away with me to Bermuda. It would show his damn Liza that he was lying about me, and about our marriage meaning nothing in his life."

25

"I'll be home early, Ann," Henry patted her hand. "And please, let's stick to Maine and scratch Bermuda."

A great contempt scattered all her previous attitudes. He wasn't worth playing tug-of-war over with this seedy Isolde of his. Let him have her—alone. And to hell with the eight years of devotion, passion, kinship. If an overnight tart could outweigh them, let her.

Ann was on her feet, her face bright with rage.

"Henry," she said, "I want to talk to you—now."

"Save it till I get home," Henry said. "I'm late now. A big fall list to go over."

"Excuse me," Hannah had shuffled in. "Two fellas from the police wanta see Mr. Lawrence. Cops. They come in without bein' asked."

Henry kissed his wife on the forehead.

"Tickets for the policeman's ball," he smiled. "You take care of them, darling. I've got to run."

He walked into the living room. Two sturdy-looking men, one young and one middle-aged, were standing near the hallway.

"Mrs. Lawrence will talk to you," Henry said.

"We want to talk to you, Mr. Lawrence," the middle-aged detective said. "My name's MacFarland and this is Sergeant Davies. We're from police headquarters. New York."

Ann had followed Henry. She knew the two men were not selling benefit tickets.

"Talk to me?" Henry frowned. "What about?"

"Do you know a man named Thomas Sovey?" asked the elderly MacFarland.

26

"Not personally," said Henry.

"You never met him, eh?" the detective asked.

"No."

"Never saw him?"

"No."

Ann wondered why he wasn't angry at these pointless questions.

"Where were you last night, Mr. Lawrence, let's say after 12:30 A.M.?" asked the detective.

"I don't understand why my whereabouts should be of any interest to the police," Henry said. "If you are police."

Both men politely showed their identification wallets. Ann waited for a curtain to go up and some unimaginable drama to begin. The other one spoke, the blond and stocky one.

"Around 12:30 A.M. this morning," said Sergeant Davies, "were you sitting in the lobby of the San Mareno Hotel on Forty-fifth Street near Broadway, Mr. Lawrence?"

"Yes," said Henry.

"Is that where Thomas Sovey lives, do you know?"

"Yes."

"Were you waiting in the lobby for Thomas Sovey to appear?" the sergeant asked.

Henry hesitated but said yes again.

"He's frightened," thought Ann. "Something awful has happened." Her large eyes looked at him. He was as mysterious as the policemen. How little of a man a woman marries! A few of his kisses and sleeping hours. She had never heard of the San Mareno Hotel or of a Mr. Sovey. Or

27

of Henry, she added suddenly. He was an alien who lived in a foreign country called Mr. Lawrence.

She heard Sergeant Davies' voice and looked at him furtively. He was a blond, blue-eyed, broad-shouldered man with a low-pitched voice. He had thick hands.

"What happened?" the sergeant asked.

"Nothing."

"Did you see Sovey?"

"No," said Henry.

Both policemen looked at him as if they had run out of questions. The silence made Henry continue talking.

"I waited for Sovey till a quarter to one. And then told the clerk to tell Mr. Sovey I'd been there, waiting for him. And I left."

The detectives stayed silent.

"What's all this about?" Henry asked. His eyes avoided his wife.

"You went straight home from the San Mareno Hotel," said MacFarland. Ann was glad this one was talking again. She could look at his face when he spoke.

"Yes, I did," said Henry.

"You didn't meet Thomas Sovey after you left the San Mareno Hotel?" the detective asked patiently. Henry didn't answer. Instead, he looked angrily at the two men. Ann knew it was a feigned anger. She feared the policemen would notice that his anger was a lie.

"Now, come, gentlemen," Henry said sharply. "I've answered a lot of senseless questions rather patiently. Before

I answer any more I want to know why you are in my home and why you're talking to me."

"Mr. Sovey was found shot to death," said MacFarland, "in an alley near the San Mareno Hotel."

"Oh," said Henry. "Sovey's dead."

"The body was found around 5:00 A.M.," said MacFarland. "He'd been dead three or four hours."

Henry was silent. Ann watched him, and wished he would sit down.

"Did you kill Sovey?" MacFarland asked.

The familiar room became incredible in Ann's eyes. Henry became incredible, as if the question had changed him vitally. After a long pause, MacFarland repeated his question. "Did you kill Thomas Sovey?"

"I didn't kill Sovey," said Henry. "I never saw him."

Ann held his arm tightly. He was trembling.

"Henry," she whispered, trying not to sound stern or frightened, "who is Thomas Sovey?"

He looked at her, painfully. "My God," she thought, "He's sorry for me, not for himself. He doesn't want to hurt me. Then it must be something about her. Damn her dirty soul," she swore in her silence. "Who cares about her? If Henry is innocent, the bitch Liza King is a minor fret. And nothing else. So he laid a blowsy girl! Who cares? He *is* innocent," she thought. "All he's worried about is hurting me.

"Who is Thomas Sovey?" she asked again. The policemen were silent.

"Mr. Sovey is, or was, a friend of someone I know," he answered.

"Henry, don't worry about me," she said. He frowned at her. It must be something involving that strumpet of his. A pox on her coarse black hair. Spreading trouble around her like a squid. Henry didn't answer. He was no longer an urbane police suspect. He seemed to have lost interest in their visitors. A sickness was in his eyes. He stood looking at her with the truculence of a cornered husband.

"Tom Sovey was a friend of Liza King," Sergeant Davies said. "Did you know her, Mrs. Lawrence?"

The blond sergeant with the thick hands made her shiver. Her instinct warned her not to answer him, or let him look in her eyes for answers. She turned away, her chin raised. Henry was in trouble over Liza King. "I must say something," she thought, "do something to protect him."

MacFarland repeated the blond sergeant's question. "Mrs. Lawrence, do you know Liza King?"

She heard herself answering this time. "Oh, yes, Miss King. She's a friend of ours. We admire her singing very much."

She stopped. She was obviously talking like an idiot in their eyes. But it didn't matter. Nor did this absurd business of Henry's having supposedly murdered a Tom Sovey matter. What mattered was that the name Liza King had finally exploded between them—and blown Liza to Hell and gone out of his life. She didn't know how this had happened, but she felt almost merry with the certainty that the New York Police Department had restored her husband to her.

She smiled at Henry, loyally. But Henry gave her back no smile. He seemed to be sneering at her. He was, she knew, reading her mind and finding it outrageous. He sensed her elation. He knew that his arrest as an alleged murderer meant nothing to her compared to the knowledge that his romance with Miss King was receiving possibly a fatal blow.

"Let him think what he wants," she thought, and returned the anger in his eyes with a mocking look that said she was very pleased indeed.

"You say you never saw Sovey last night?" Sergeant Davies asked.

"I never saw him in my life," Henry answered.

"But you knew all about him, didn't you?"

Henry hesitated. "Yes," he said.

"What did you know?" the blond sergeant asked.

Again the hesitation. "He doesn't want to talk in front of me." Tears suddenly filled her eyes as she added, "Oh, God, he's ashamed."

"Sovey was a drunken, out-of-work actor," Henry said, "who was bothering Miss King a great deal. He was always trying to borrow money from her on the strength of—a previous relationship."

Sergeant Davies smiled and looked boldly at Ann.

"He's a hateful man," she glared at the sergeant. "He likes to hurt people."

"You mean, Sovey was trying to get her back as his sweetie, don't you?" Sergeant Davies asked.

"No."

"As a matter of fact," the blond sergeant said, "you were

31

sore as hell at this Sovey and jealous of him, weren't you?"

Ann turned away again from the low-voiced sergeant. She didn't want to hear what he went on saying. Henry jealous of a cheap drunken actor. Quarreling with Liza King over him. Shouting at her that she was being untrue to him with some broken-down sot. How low could a man sink? A man like Henry.

"We understand that Tom Sovey was also trying to blackmail you," Sergeant Davies said. "He threatened to tell your wife about you and Liza King unless you bought him off. Is that true?"

"It's not true," said Henry. Ann knew he was lying.

"We understand you had a fight with Miss King last night," Sergeant Davies said. "You accused her of two-timing you with Sovey. Is that true?"

"Is what true?" Henry asked.

"Did she two-time you?" Davies asked.

"He's trapping him in some way," thought Ann. "Shall I call up Sam Hartnett?" she asked aloud. Sam was their best friend and a brilliant lawyer.

"No," said Henry.

"We understand that Sovey called up Miss King's apartment while you were with her last night," said Davies, "and that you got into a fight with her over him. Is that correct, Mr. Lawrence?"

"Yes," said Henry, and Ann felt a deeper victory. The police must have gotten their information from Liza King. A fine, loyal lover Miss King had turned out to be. Throwing Henry to the dogs. Telling everything to the police. "A cheap, unscrupulous tart," Ann thought, "the kind men like to play sexual mud pies with." She felt almost magnanimous, like a successful candidate whom the voters had continued in office.

"Did you quarrel with Miss King over any other men?" Davies asked. The man spoke as if he were apologizing for breaking a silence. But there was no apology in his half-hidden eyes.

"That's none of your God damn business," Henry said.

"Other men," Ann thought. "My God, she's probably a call girl with a large clientele. What the hell have I been worrying about? No Isolde, that bitch."

In the midst of her bitter satisfaction, Ann's heart contracted with terror. Henry was answering the blond policeman's question but his words blurred in her ears. She was looking at his muffler hanging from the couch arm. It was stained. "Bloodstains," she thought.

She moved to the couch and sat down slowly, as if overcome by what she was hearing. The muffler disappeared under her. Neither of the policemen noticed its vanishing.

"We had a number of discussions about Sovey," Henry finished his answer, "but I never saw him."

"Why did you go to the San Mareno Hotel?" Detective MacFarland asked.

"I told you I never saw him."

"That wasn't what I asked," said the detective. "Why'd you go to his hotel and sit an hour waiting for him?"

"To talk to him, obviously," said Henry.

"Wasn't it your intention to beat him up?" MacFarland asked.

"I think we've got enough," Sergeant Davies said.

"Do you care to answer the question?" MacFarland waited.

"I never saw Sovey or beat him up or shot him," said Henry. Ann closed her eyes. He was lying. They could hear the lie, as well as she could. The way he emphasized the words, as if he were making a speech.

"Where's the tan topcoat you wore last night?" Mac-Farland asked.

"Bloodstains on his coat, too," Ann thought, and the familiar room darkened as if the morning had become full of storm. But she remained sitting upright on the muffler.

Sergeant Davies said, "You'll have to come along with us, Mr. Lawrence."

MacFarland returned from the hallway with a topcoat over his arm.

"We'll take this along, too," he said.

"I want to talk to my wife alone," Henry said.

"We'll wait in the hall," MacFarland said. The two detectives walked out of the room.

"How long have you known about Liza?" he asked softly.

"Does it matter now?" she whispered.

She wanted to say that nothing mattered beside his danger, that she was his ally despite a hundred Liza Kings. He looked at her as if he, too, wanted to say something.

"That he loves me," Ann thought eagerly. "No, he thinks

34

I'm still gloating. He doesn't realize that girl is a thing of the past. Already forgotten."

"It's an involved story," Henry said, and sighed. "And I'm sort of glad it's finally in the open. For everybody's sake."

Not for her sake. Not because they could be the old Ann and Henry again, with no rotten lies between them. Why was he glad, then? And about what?

"You knew about Liza for some time?" he said.

"Yes," she took his hand. It felt icy. "For some time." Nine days could be called "some time."

"I wish you'd told me," she added.

"It's the sort of thing one hesitates to tell a wife." Banter was back in his voice.

"I can imagine," she smiled.

"You're amazing," he said.

"Why?"

"I expected a major demonstration," he answered.

"That—thing, I mean your Liza didos," she was using his words, "don't matter any more."

"Thanks," said Henry, "for not adding to the present annoyance."

He squeezed her hand.

"If you love me," she began.

He nodded. "I love you."

"It doesn't matter then, at all."

"I hope not," he said.

"I'll call up Sam. He can clear everything up, legally. I mean—with the police."

"Darling," he smiled at her, "you're fine. But don't try to help me too much. I've got to do things my way."

"What things, darling?"

"All kinds of upside-down things," he answered.

The two policemen came to the doorway.

"We better get going," said the blond sergeant. He looked at Ann. "I may want to ask you some questions this afternoon, ma'am," Sergeant Davies said from the door. "Will you be here?"

She nodded.

The door closed behind the three men. Pale, dizzy, Ann was still sitting on the muffler.

Two days of sharp activity followed, as if life had become a race instead of a walk. Henry's good friend and lawyer Sam Hartnett was at her side during most of the speeding hours. Despite his sincerity and eagerness, Ann found friend Sam a difficult companion. She always had. His puffy, boyish face, his budding paunch and thinning hair were almost a second self of Henry—she had seen them together so much. And if not with Sam, she had seen him with Elsie. If Henry and Elsie found Sam palatable and even diverting, it was mean of her to look on him always as a bore. A tall, blondish, blue-eyed, kindly man, she told herself, and a brilliant lawyer. They were riding in a taxicab.

"I'll have the sonofagun out on bail," Sam said, "as soon as I can pound some sense into the D.A.'s head."

"I have complete confidence in you, Sam," Ann said.

"Thanks," Sam patted her hand. His hand was puffy like his face, and he had no ankles. The hair on his wrists was blond. But it wasn't Sam's physical flaws that made her wince as they rode together. It was his drooling devotion to his "bride." Ten years of marriage had failed to provide him with another name for Elsie.

"Heard from my bride up in Maine this morning," he said, "a wonderful telegram."

"You read it to me," Ann said.

"What a woman," said Sam. His pale blue eyes filled with mood, like an actor's.

"She's a dear," said Ann, and thought, "He's like some fat cow mooing." She looked at him quickly. Fat cow? It couldn't be that Sam, one of Englewood's most esteemed citizens, was a homosexual? Or even half a one? No, he was much worse than that. He was the ironed-out suburbia-male, a sort of tomb of platitudes, and always the fearless champion of the obvious. But there must be more than that to Sam, or how could Elsie love him and Henry call him best friend?

"I talked to Elsie this morning on the phone," said Sam. "God, I miss my bride when she's that far away. Imagine, Maine! I told her the police have no case whatsoever against Henry."

"Then why is he in jail?" Ann's tears started.

37

"There, there," Sam patted her hand again, "you're not the crying kind, Ann."

"Not often," she said.

"Good girl," said Sam. "Elsie always says you're as tough as a Marine sergeant." He smiled at her. "Looks are certainly deceiving."

"A cliché a minute," Ann sighed. "My God, mottoes pour out of him like out of a weighing machine." Aloud, she asked, "Please tell me why they're keeping Henry in jail—for no reason?"

"Because he's a damn fool," said Sam, "and refuses to co-operate."

"Co-operate means telling the police something damning about Liza King," she said.

"Let's put it this way," said Sam, "it means telling the simple, honest truth."

"You think he knows something about Miss King—and the murder?"

"I think," said Sam carefully, "that Henry is behaving like a college boy."

"You mean he's being gallant toward a tart," said Ann. They were out of the taxi and now in the dining room of Sam's University Club.

"A man doesn't owe any woman like that gallantry," said Sam.

Ann felt unreasonably irritated. She ate her soup without rebuttal. Sam talked on. Ann thought, "He talks as if he were constantly addressing a convention of wives." She remembered suddenly a fact about Sam. He had actually

38

betrayed Elsie with a skinny, watery-eyed secretary. And been caught sexually occupied with her in his office after hours, and by Elsie in person. My God, what a dithering hypocrite he was. Or like some oily convert to morality whose every syllable must testify for his reform.

"We'll talk to Henry together," Sam said, toward the end of the lunch.

"No," said Ann. "I want to see him alone. You can see him after I've talked to him."

"It may be a little unpleasant for you, Ann. A man in jail is liable to show his worst side."

"I'm quite used to Henry's worst side," Ann said. "He's a depraved, unscrupulous male, and he was born that way. Men never change," she looked accusingly at Sam, "even in jail."

Sam answered admiringly, "Elsie is right. You're a real Marine. Tough as they come."

"I'm not a Marine," Ann said as she stood up. "I weigh one hundred and twelve pounds and have a very tender skin."

"Elsie ought to see you now!" said Sam. "I don't think you ever looked more beautiful."

An hour later, a guard led Ann upstairs to Henry's cell block. She was told to wait in front of a wire mesh wall.

After a few minutes, Henry appeared on the other side of the mesh. The guard stood fifteen feet away.

"Hello," said Henry. "Nice of you to drop in."

"I'm not interrupting?" Ann smiled.

"No, I was just sitting around," said Henry.

His manner worried her. Why was he acting for her? "My God," she thought suddenly, "what if he's guilty. How do I know anything about him?"

"Darling," she said, "Sam and I have talked everything over."

"Where is that bumbling barrister?"

"I insisted on seeing you alone. Sam thinks you're an utter nitwit for withholding information from the police."

"I'm withholding nothing."

A lie in his most obvious liar's voice. She continued, "I can quite understand male gallantry. On the other hand, I dislike seeing you go to the electric chair, however gallantly."

"That's quite a long way off," said Henry.

"Darling," Ann said, "she's told the police every damning detail she could about you. I'm not talking as a bruised wife." She smiled. "I've changed for the better, Henry. I'm your lover and best friend."

"My congratulations," Henry was sarcastic.

"I know you're innocent," Ann ignored his tone. "You could no more kill anyone than pick somebody's pocket. You're too oral for crime without words."

"Thank you," said Henry, "you'll make a good witness."

"Please, Henry, be sensible. You're not going to help Miss King any by sitting in jail. Like a tongue-tied idiot."

"Let's not talk about Miss King," said Henry. "She doesn't bring out the best in either of us."

"The police know you're lying about her," said Ann.

"The police bore me," Henry said.

"There's no sense in your telling lies to save her," Ann said. "Because if she's guilty, your idiotic lies won't help her a bit, and if she isn't guilty, she'll be able to prove it without your having to rot in jail for her."

"Can we take up some other topic?" Henry asked.

"You're thoroughly rotten," said Ann.

"What man isn't?" Henry sighed.

"Henry, I don't want to talk about Miss King any more than you do, but we must."

"I disagree," said Henry.

"I don't mean about your contemptible affair with her," said Ann. "I have utterly no interest in that."

"At this time," Henry smiled.

"But your college-boy theatrics to save her are utterly stupid," she said.

Henry sighed patiently.

"Unless, of course, you're madly in love with her," Ann said, "and want her to realize the depths of your great passion. Oh, what a rotten man you are!"

"Please," said Henry. "It's unfair to harass a man in jail. I wouldn't act this way toward you if you were sitting in a prison cell full of cockroaches."

"Oh, shut up!" said Ann. "You make me sick with your fake attitudes."

But he didn't. She wanted to be in his arms, kissing him. The antic note in his voice thrilled her. He was a villain unmasked, yet his unmasking left him unchanged. "The heroics of villainy," she thought. They were somehow more attractive than the heroics of virtue.

Henry was saying, "I'm sorry to be cranky under the circumstances. But please keep out of my hair. You and Sam, both." He disappeared. Ann called his name through the wire mesh but he remained invisible.

Walking out of the prison building, Ann thought, "He's stubborn and stupid." But she continued to admire him as if he were quite something else. Over the phone, she said to Sam Hartnett, "I couldn't get anything out of him. He talks like a nine-year-old. Booth Tarkington's 'Penrod' under a cloud. Do try to get him out, Sam."

"May I say," said Sam, "that next to Elsie you're the most remarkable woman I've ever known."

Ann went home. Driving, she thought, "He's treating it as a half joke. But what if he and his joke go to trial? And things turn out wrong?" Fear came into her. "He isn't an idiot," she thought, "and he's *not* joking. It's no joke to go to jail. With all Englewood gloating. And his business hurt. No, it's something real. He knows something horribly real—that the woman killed Sovey. And he can't bring himself to tattle on her and send her to prison for life. Or worse. A man like Henry can't do that. Even if he hated the woman. And he doesn't hate her."

Her admiration for Henry's heroics disappeared. She entered her home. The slippered Hannah hovered over the dining table as if it were a deathbed.

"How is the mister?" she asked.

"He seems to be quite pleased with himself," Ann said.

"That's the way he is," old Hannah nodded, "but he loves you, modom. I cut my head off on that."

"Any phone calls?" Ann asked.

"Lots," said Hannah, and shuffled out of the room.

In bed, Ann lay looking at the moon over Englewood. She tried to think of a number of things—the scurrilous seminars on the Lawrences going on among their friends, the eagerness to mourn over other people's misfortunes, particularly if they were bright people like Henry and herself. But a sort of motion picture film kept running in her mind, a pornographic film of Henry and Liza King in a bedroom. The action was unvaried. A naked Miss King crawled into a bed with a naked Henry. They embraced and the scene faded out, and started up again at the beginning.

She remembered Henry's words: "The worst thing about jealousy is that the thing you know repeats itself. Jealousy sits looking at a single incident. The crime committed against you. And the crime repeats itself. It keeps yelling at you like one of those damnably unvarying commercials on television."

How did he know? Of whom had Henry been jealous? Never of her.

A thought excited her. The film stopped running. "I've got to see Liza King and talk to her. That's the only way.

She killed that man. I can find it all out by talking to her. A woman can find out."

But how talk to Liza King? Miss King would sneer at any quizzing wife. Women like Liza looked on wives the way gangsters did on cops. No possible communication, except bloodshed or hair pulling.

In the breakfast nook, Ann left the morning papers unopened. Oddly, Henry's deviltry in print had no interest for her. Possibly because it contained no information or insight. As she ate, she talked to Henry almost as if he were at the table. "Good lord," she thought, "my mind is hardly more than an echo of that rotten man."

Old Hannah insisted she eat another batch of toast because she needed strength.

"I don't need any strength, Hannah. And please stop looking at me as if I were on a slab in the morgue."

Hannah exited like a funeral march. She remembered Henry's words: "Wives are always strong. Because they think they're always in the right." Yes, that's the way she had always thought. More from the invisible Henry: "A good husband is a man who can consistently pretend to be what his wife thinks he is. It's like learning to hop on one leg, when you're a kid." And another time, at a dinner party with five grimly staring and silent wives: "Women have a wonderful habit of mistaking their demands for gifts. Particularly wives. The more you give a wife, the more you owe her. That's always the way when righteousness keeps the books."

Ann thought at her breakfast, "How could I have been

44

such an idiot as to enjoy all his denunciations of wifehood? As if I weren't involved. But it was me he was talking about all the time. What a fool I must have seemed to everybody, applauding him. And arguing with other wives how right he was." The time he had said, about husbands, "Wives are our external consciences with a little whorish equipment." And Elsie had demanded an apology. "Forgive me," said Henry, "for minimizing your equipment. It's terrific." That was a strange apology, and stranger still, Elsie had accepted it. Obviously all women were too addleheaded to notice the meaning of words. A flattering tone was enough to content them.

Ann felt the victim-pain ebb in her nerves, the pain of being a betrayed and scandalized wife. Being on Henry's "side" lessened the pain of his crime against her. She thought, "I mustn't think, act or feel like a wife. At least while he's in jail. Or I'll be useless to Henry. If I want to help him—" A happy surge of loyalty filled her. But she must be careful about harassing him with her loyalty. An erring husband doesn't want wifely loyalty—at least not the loquacious kind.

"He doesn't want anything from me," she thought, "but he wants something from Liza King. Her approval and admiration. He's showing off for her, and enjoying it in his own cynical way. But maybe he's sincere and doing something rather noble. I mustn't keep looking down on him. Only a wife does that. I'm his lover and friend. He could be frightened. The thought of destroying Liza King by telling the police on her probably sickens him. Poor Henry,

I'll see that girl. I'll make her talk—somehow. I know I can."

Hannah announced the arrival of Sergeant Davies and Detective MacFarland. It was the latter who asked the questions. But she kept looking at the broad-shouldered, heavy-handed blond sergeant. Her skin wrinkled with aversion. The man seemed to purr in his silence, and his eyes never opened fully.

"The hotel clerk described your husband wearing a white muffler last night," said MacFarland. "We didn't see it in the hall closet."

"I haven't the faintest notion of where my husband keeps his muffler," said Ann.

"You didn't happen to see it when you came down that morning?" the detective asked.

"I did not," said Ann. "May I ask what possible interest Mr. Lawrence's muffler can have for you?"

"Just that it seems to be missing," said the detective.

"You are welcome to look through the house," said Ann.

"That won't be necessary." The blond one spoke in his low voice. "We'll take your word for it, that it isn't on the premises."

"I don't know where it is. I don't know anything about it." Ann's voice rose. "And please leave me alone. You have no right bothering me."

"Our apologies," said Sergeant Davies.

She looked at his insistent physique. He bulged his coat like an athlete. But he seemed alien and unfriendly. His thick hands revolted her.

"Did Tom Sovey ever talk to you in person or over the telephone?" he asked.

"No," she glared at him.

"On the night Sovey was killed," Davies asked, "did you hear your husband telephone Miss King after he got home?"

So Liza had told that to the police also.

"No, I was asleep."

"You sure?" Davies asked.

"Yes, I'm very sure," Ann said. She thought, "He knows I'm lying. And he wants me to lie, I can feel him. He wants to mix me up. I hate him."

Aloud, she said, "I'm not going to answer any more of your questions, Sergeant Davies."

Sam Hartnett appeared like a rescue party. She greeted him eagerly, and ignored the departing policeman.

"What the devil did they want?" Sam asked.

"Oh, just questions, questions," said Ann. "Had breakfast, Sam?" He hadn't. He gabbled through eggs, toast and coffee.

"He talks like a tomato-can label," Ann thought, "but he's righteous. And that helps in anybody but a wife."

"Even if Henry were guilty," Sam munched his toast, "I'd get him off. If he co-operated."

"But he isn't guilty, Sam."

"I'm speaking as his lawyer," said Sam. "The law could never prove he shot Sovey. Motive and opportunity are not enough to remove all reasonable doubts."

As he talked on, Ann thought, "Truth doesn't mean anything to a lawyer. They're really like husbands. What they can make somebody else believe—that's truth. That's the

47

way husbands treat wives—as if they were a jury to be out-witted or hoodwinked."

"All husbands are lawyers," she said suddenly. Sam was surprised to hear this.

"In what way?" he asked cautiously.

"They're always working to get a criminal off scot free—themselves."

"My dear Ann," Sam said, "no husband ever gets off scot free." His tired, boyish face blushed. "Not to change the subject," he said, "I'd like you to meet the District Attorney today. It'll help in an oblique way."

"What do I have to do, show him my legs?" Ann asked.

"That's legitimate legal procedure," Sam smiled. "Come on, chin up, Ann."

The day passed under Sam's guidance. He hailed taxi-cabs, ushered her into offices, introduced her to various police and government officials, and guarded her from a half-dozen newspaper reporters and photographers.

Ann was annoyed at this last activity. She wanted to talk to the newspapermen, tell them her belief in Henry's inno-cence, make light of the scandalous Liza business, and hint of Liza's guilt. It would have been easy. The speeches were in her mind. "My husband is a little too gallant for his own good. He'd rather wait in jail for the police to discover without his help who really killed Tom Sovey."

But Sam wouldn't hear of it. "Not a word for publication, Ann. There's one rule about newspapers. Never talk when they're after you." It sounded mysteriously correct, and she gave in.

Home again, Ann bathed and pondered the main plot line—Liza King. She soaked in the hot water. "I can only get her to talk if I'm her friend. Or if I can make her feel friendly. But how, in God's name!" Disguise occurred to her. "Utterly stupid," she thought, "she's seen my picture in the papers."

She left the tub with the plot unsolved. An empty, desperate feeling was in her. "I love Henry," she thought, "I really do. And not as a possession. As a dear friend. It makes me sick to think of him sitting in that rotten jail."

She wondered at the phrase, "I love Henry." It had come casually into her mind. Where was yesterday's pain? "It'll come back," she sighed, "and run over me like an express train again." She shuddered. She remembered suddenly that Sam Hartnett was sitting in his large ornate home alone two blocks away, with Elsie up in Maine chasing her damn fish. The thing to do was ask Sam over for dinner— if only for Elsie's sake. She hoped to heaven Elsie would stay put in Maine. Elsie was her best friend, but no cohort for her now. Elsie was the Wives' Union, sitting in perpetual session. She wanted neither pity nor advice from that organization.

Sam arrived in fifteen minutes, beaming with gratitude. "It's always pretty lonely in that house when Elsie's away," he wrung her hand. "I just got through talking to her when you called. She sends you her love. And if there's anything she can do. She's quite a girl, Elsie. Cream puff on the outside, but real steel inside. I remember once when I was courting her—about twelve years ago—"

49

He gabbled on through dinner, switching finally from Elsie's fine qualities to his own, reciting conversations between himself and important political figures, and throwing in a few anecdotes of his boyhood on a Minnesota farm. He interrupted himself only to turn on a favorite television program—a western with an unconquerable sheriff. As talker and TV listener, he drank casually but persistently.

"What a nuisance to have around the house," Ann thought. "No wonder wives go crazy—having to listen to all that normalcy."

But Sam's normalcy began to wane. He turned off the western in its middle and said skittishly, "That sheriff is no match for you, Ann. To hell with him." He asked for another highball.

"Well, my girl," he raised his glass gallantly, "to you. A real soldier. Yes, sir, you're taking it like a real soldier. My God, there aren't many wives who'd be using their brains at a time like this. I certainly admire you, Ann."

He drank his highball like a successful orator. Ann watched his hail-fellow face and wished Hannah hadn't gone so pointedly to bed. It was nine o'clock. She poured herself a weak drink.

Two days ago she would have thought nothing of sitting alone with Sam in the middle of a dark prairie. But something odd seemed to have changed her world, as if she and not Henry had been exposed as a sinner.

"Good lord, he's frisking around me," she thought. "I can't believe it." It was like witnessing a Jekyll-Hyde transformation. The loyal, devoted husband growing lustful fangs. "He's giving off signals. If I wish to avenge myself for Henry's infidelity he's willing to offer more than legal co-operation. What an oaf! How can he even imagine such a thing? But they're all oafs, all men. The way they looked at me today. A wife with a broken heart is obviously fair game. Almost as easy pickings as a call girl."

The phone rang. It was long-distance.

"Hello," said Elsie from Maine. "I'm so worried about you. How are you, darling?"

"Bearing up," said Ann.

"I've half a mind to come back to New York and be at your side," said Elsie.

"That's not necessary," said Ann. "But thank you, darling. It'll blow over in a day or so."

"I'm sure it will," said Elsie. "With Sam handling it. Please rely on him for everything, Ann. He's much brighter than he looks. And he adores Henry. Always has."

Ann turned to call Sam to the phone. He was not in the room.

"I will, darling. How's the fishing?"

"Nothing," said Elsie. "I don't see why we come up here year after year. There hasn't been a fish in these waters since the Civil War."

The talk continued for several minutes. Elsie was a staunch friend. And wise, in a curious way. "Don't mind what our silly friends have to say," Elsie said. "They just love to feel sorry for people. It's much more fun than feel-ing sorry for themselves. And, darling, they're all, secretly, very dirty people. You're much too innocent to know, but

51

take my word for it. Englewood is an utterly filthy place."

Finally Ann said, "Good-by, darling. And thanks for your loyal words. You must tell me about Englewood's sex underground. I really am in the dark there. No, please don't ask any questions about Henry. I don't want to make any answer yet. You *do* understand?"

"Of course I do," said Elsie. "Henry is a wretched, vicious man and you adore him. Darling, if he were my husband I'd get into that jail and break his neck."

"I may do that yet," said Ann. "Good-by, darling."

She looked around again. Sam appeared.

"That was Elsie," she said.

"I know," he looked roguish. "I wasn't in the mood to talk to her again. You didn't tell her I was here?"

"No," said Ann, and wondered why she hadn't.

"I don't like those cops bothering you," Sam frowned. "I'm going to talk to the Commissioner tomorrow." Sam never talked to anybody but top echelon people.

She thought of the bloodstained muffler that had taken thirty minutes to burn in the furnace. She should tell Sam about it. She could trust him but the evening was becoming confusing. It was no longer a legal evening. And his running out when Elsie was on the phone. The conference was beginning to look more like a courtship. She watched Sam pour another highball. He had a wistful look. "And he's scared," Ann thought, "of his lecherous attitude toward me. And of me, too. Whether I'll tell Elsie. He's terrified of Elsie. What a silly fellow."

"The way you handled yourself today," Sam beamed, "was a revelation in feminine charm and class."

"I didn't show my legs too much?"

"You couldn't show those legs too much, my dear," he studied her knees. "By George, you're the kind of a gal a man doesn't meet up with often. Beautiful, classy, and likewise smart as a whip."

Ann put on her most Englewood look, a combination of innocence and social amusement. "The smile of suburbia," Henry called it, "to be found only on social leaders and incarcerated idiots." But Sam was going to require more than an innocent stare to keep him at bay. The thing to do was send him home. Letting him frisk around her in this fashion was black disloyalty to Elsie. Elsie who glowed with wifely security, come wind, come rain. Elsie, up in Maine, but as sure of her Sam as if he were tattooed on her forearm. What idiots wives were!

Starting a shooing-home speech, Ann stopped and her heart beat with sudden purpose. She knew how to make friends with Liza King. Utterly simple. No disguises. Just a little acting. She'd call on Liza King and bring Sam along as her lover. Put on a big infidelity act with Sam as her paramour. All she had to do was pour liquor into him, and not slap his face. And Sam would play his part to the hilt.

"It's perfect," Ann thought, "she'd only laugh and sneer at an honest wife. But she'd get a thrill out of meeting a two-timing Mrs. Lawrence, on the town with her lover boy. Especially after what Henry must have told her. What a wifely stick I am. A puritanical policeman." Other wife

epithets favored by Henry came to her. Liza King had prob-
ably heard all of them. "Good. She'll be happily surprised.
And she'll talk to a deceiving wife, heading for the hay with
Sam. Because I'll be like her. And Henry. Birds of a feather.
It's perfect."

Sam was talking in a low, intimate voice. He was telling
a dirty story. She smiled encouragingly, and tried to keep
herself attentive enough to laugh at the point, if it ever
arrived. Sam was a detailed talker. He took a long time
getting to the worried spinster starting to undress in the
room without knowing her nephew was hiding under the
bed.

Sipping her drink as he ambled on, Ann thought, "I'll
keep him going when he starts making a pass at me. Up to a
point. A few kisses aren't going to hurt anybody. My God,
I'm not a virgin."

Ann winced slightly. The thought of some other man's
kisses had never come to her before. Had she lost her decency along with Henry, the way people seemed to hint
when they smiled condolences at her? How was she different from Liza King, plotting now to attract somebody's
husband? "Oh, I'm being stupid," she thought, "Liza King
worked only for herself. I'll be doing it for Henry to prove
his innocence. And," she added quickly, "I won't be doing
much. Just a sort of beginning."

She joined Sam's laughter, without having caught the
point of his dirty story.

"Oh, that's very funny," she said.

Sam sat down facing her, knees to knees. An odd position

for courtship, she thought. But Sam wasn't courting yet. Or possibly he was—lawyer fashion.

"Now here's the case to date," he said, his knees firmly against hers. "The police figure that Sovey was blackmailing Henry. Threatening to tell you about his Liza King affair. And that Sovey was also trying to get back in that young lady's good graces and elsewhere." Sam winked. "And they figure that Henry met Sovey in the alley, after he left the San Mareno Hotel, and got into a filthy row with him. And that Henry lost his head and fired the fatal shot."

"But Henry never owned a gun," she frowned. "I've told that horrid Sergeant Davies. Truly, Sam, he never did."

"As far as you know," Sam nodded. "And, as a matter of fact, I'm inclined to agree with you. If worst comes to worst, with a little help from Henry, I can defend him against manslaughter. And prove self-defense. It was Sovey who pulled the gun. Henry wrestled with him. And the gun went off in the scrimmage."

"Sam," she leaned forward, "Henry denies having even seen Sovey."

"I know," Sam said, "that's his present story."

"I believe him."

Sam smiled tenderly. "I should think by this time you'd have realized that Henry is not a fountain of truth."

"I believe him," she repeated, "because—" She stared openmouthed at a memory. "Oh, my God, I've just remembered something. Of course he's innocent! It's obvious!"

"What is it?"

"That damn detective put it out of my mind by making

me lie about it," she smiled eagerly. "What Henry said on the phone when he came home. Tuesday morning. He called her up. And I listened to something that proves he's innocent. Wait, I must remember it!"

"Perhaps I can help you." Sam's courtroom manner was rather thrilling—forceful and relaxing. "You say he was talking to Miss King?" She nodded. "You're sure of that?" She nodded again. "Where were you standing, Ann?"

"I was hidden on the landing."

"And you could hear plainly?"

"Too plainly."

"No emotion now," Sam said. "Just put yourself back in that place. Close your eyes and try to remember the conversation you heard."

"I can't, Sam," she stood up quickly and reached for his arm, eagerly. "It's been driven out of my mind. But I'll remember it. You must believe me. I've been worrying so about the bloodstained muffler. And whether I'd done right in burning it up."

"The bloodstained muffler!" Sam said. "Good God! Whose?"

"Henry's."

"He came home Tuesday 2:00 A.M. with a bloodstained muffler?" Sam stared at her.

"Yes."

"And you burned it up?"

"Yes."

Sam turned away, scowling. "I wish you hadn't told me,"

he said. "I'm a lawyer, Ann. I have a certain responsibility. Destroying evidence is a criminal act."

"I'm sorry," she said, and squeezed his muscular arm.

"How do you know they were bloodstains?"

"They looked like them."

"Lots of things look like bloodstains," Sam frowned. "Including bloodstains."

"That muffler would only have clouded the issue," she said, "and made it harder to prove his innocence. But you're right. I'm sorry I told you. It slipped out because I forgot you were a lawyer. I thought of you as—a friend."

"I am. I'm your friend, first, last and foremost," said Sam. "There's nothing I wouldn't do for you, Ann—nothing. But let's, for his sake, tackle this thing reasonably. He came home with a bloodstained muffler, and you think he's innocent—because of something you can't remember. By God, it was tough enough trying to cook up a story of what happened to Sovey's gun after the accidental or self-defense shooting. But this is worse—trying to prove a man's innocence by his wife's faulty memory—and loyal conviction." He smiled at her tenderly. "Ann, you're a great girl. You're just wonderful. And so damned sweet."

"It came to me as I was falling asleep last night." She refilled both their highball glasses. "It seems years ago. I had to take two pills. They made my mind fuzzy. I remembered his calling her. And just as I was falling asleep I remembered that I'd heard something that proves his innocence."

"Did he mention the name Sovey?" Sam asked quickly.

"No."

"Was it because he seemed in good spirits—unlike a man who'd killed somebody?"

"Oh, he was happy enough," she answered. "But that wouldn't prove anything. It's not that. Damn, damn, damn. Why can't I remember it?"

"Some sort of psychic stoppage," said Sam. "Maybe Henry can help us there. I'll ask him for the full phone conversation with Miss King tomorrow."

"Don't."

"Why not?"

"I don't want him to know I was spying on him."

"You had every right to, Ann."

"He's angry at me enough now, Sam."

"He's angry at you! Well, he's got a fine right to be angry! If I were in his place I'd be on my hands and knees to you begging to be forgiven."

Ann remembered the finale Elsie had reported for the Vassar graduate bacchanalia—Sam had gone on his hands and knees and wept for forgiveness.

"Maybe my fine husband doesn't want to be forgiven," she said.

"Don't be silly," he grinned. "All husbands do. A husband who doesn't want to be forgiven is just being unnecessarily cruel. And ratty."

Ann pondered this. They had sat down again, this time closely side by side.

"Although I'll admit," he went on, "that Henry's a little

unusual. He's not the ordinary husband. We've had a lot of talks about marriage."

"He doesn't believe in it," Ann smiled.

"That's right," Sam stared at her. "I didn't want to say it behind his back. But, as long as you know, he always said—"

"That marriage was a species of mutual blackmail," she finished Sam's dragging sentence. "And that it only had one virtue. If husbands and wives hung onto each other long enough, they ended by having something vitally in common—a misspent life."

She felt a return of the victim-pain as she remembered Henry's sprightly cynicisms. She wondered why and knew the answer. They hinted that there had been others before Liza King. She couldn't be sure. She had always accepted his antimoral attitudes as part of their love and mutual companionship; it was difficult to believe they had all been cunning warnings given off by a chronic philanderer. "I mustn't start guessing," she thought. "I'll end up putting him in the right by a lot of mis-accusations." She thought of Henry holding forth on his favorite topic to Liza King. My God, how he must have babbled to her about the horrors of wedlock!

"I haven't changed as much as I hoped," she sighed inwardly. "I guess, once a wife, always a wife."

"After the way you loved him," Sam said tenderly, "it's unbelievable for a man to talk like that. By God, I've never known a more perfect wife! As for a woman as beautiful as you to stay true blue to a man and then have him behave as

59

Henry's behaving—as if he were in the right. After what he's done to you! My God, I call it unpardonable. Even though he *is* my best friend. Crude and unpardonable. And I don't mean this Liza business. Every man slips up once in a while. Although how a man could want to step out when he had you in his bed. Good Lord! Unbelievable! But I'm sore at Henry for this one other thing. The main thing. His indifference to how horribly he's hurt you."

Sam ran out of breath. "The sales talk," Ann thought. "From here on it's concentrated pawing." A small fear made her shiver. Could she stand another man's physical touch? His lips? Hands? "I'm nearly drunk," she thought. "If it gets too much I can pretend to pass out. No. No passing out. I've got to get him to Liza—full of original sin." She watched Sam's face. It was a boy's face, full of dedication, as if it were playing some fascinating game.

"I'll get that smart husband of yours out of this," said Sam, "as soon as I can convince him to stop lying about having met Sovey. And plead self-defense."

He was on his feet fetching drinks.

"You won't like what I'm going to say, Ann, but it's too late for kidding ourselves. The reason Henry's lying about everything is Liza King. He's all wrapped up in what she thinks. Not what you and I think. It's one of those infatuations. I've seen a lot of smart men lose their heads like that."

He came back, two glasses in hand. "Here, join me, and let's forget everybody's troubles for a minute."

She took the glass nervously. He sat down on the arm of her chair.

60

"I know how awful you must feel," he said, "despite the front you're putting up. By God, how a man can trade you in for a cheap little tramp like Liza King. I'd understand it if it was just for a day or two. But a love affair! With all the trimmings! That's unbelievable!"

"He's trying to make me cry," Ann thought, "so as to have an excuse for putting his arm around me." She finished her drink and looked up at him with tear-wetted eyes. The arm came around her shoulder.

"Go on, cry," Sam said huskily. "It'll do you good."

His hand on her shoulder was moist and vibrant—a hand full of ideas. She thought, "This is the way it begins. Henry's best friend and Elsie's best friend. Half fried. And ready to— Oh, no. Not to bed. That isn't necessary. I'll just try to keep him loving."

"You've got the most beautiful hair and eyes of any woman I've ever seen," Sam said. His hands moved gently over her hair, bringing a tingle into her nerves. It was pleasant to have a man trembling for you again. "How polite they are while still in the trembling stage," she thought. The movie of Liza and Henry in their first embrace started running in her mind.

She closed her eyes. She felt half drunk and full of sudden emotion. Her new unwifely self disappeared. She wanted to cry over Henry's perfidy, over his betrayal and abandonment of her. Over his love for another woman. A horrid, empty woman. "I loved him so," she said to her heart, "how could he do it? How? To me? After all our wild passion. After those thousand nights. To throw me away." The crime, Henry's crime, repeated itself freshly in her thought. As if it had just happened. And all its horror was in her.

Sam was holding her avidly. They had stood up—at just what point in her grief, she couldn't remember. Kisses held her mouth silent. Elsie was in Maine. Henry was in a police cell pining for his fat-lipped Liza. The kissing gained momentum. "Oh, God," she thought, "I must remember it's not Henry." But the thought seemed to increase rather than lessen her sensual abandon. An elation she had never felt in Henry's arms filled her body as if it were running away from her. "I'm going to do it," she thought happily. Sam broke the spell. He lessened the pressure of his body in order to put his emptied glass on the table. She stepped quickly away.

"Sam, dear," she began, not knowing what to say. Her senses were still beating with his ardor and her own. No one but Henry had ever touched and kissed her in that erotic fashion. And she had responded more than if it were Henry. Still dizzied, she realized dimly that her body was more trained to lechery than her soul to virtue—as what wife's isn't. "My God," she thought, "I'm not me. I could love anybody."

Sam interrupted. "You're beautiful," he said. His voice was hoarse. "You drive me completely crazy."

"Not again—now," she held him away. "Sam, I need your help. Please help me."

"Anything," said Sam, and moved in quickly like a wrestler. He could use both arms and hands this time.

"Oh, no, please, not now," she protested under his kisses. There must be some magic word to stop both of them.

"Elsie," she panted against his mouth.

"She's in Maine," said Sam hoarsely.

"Oh, my God," she tried another tack and went limp in his arms as if consciousness had fled. Sam held her limp body erect with one arm, and fumbled with the front of her dress with his free hand.

"You need air," he said gruffly.

"Please, Sam dear," she kept her voice weak, "you said you'd help me."

"Anything," Sam kissed away at her neck. She surprised him by taking his face in her hands, as if it were Henry's face and she was going to kiss it abandonedly. Instead, she twisted out of his unwary arms. She smiled and raised her handkerchief to his lips.

"Don't move. Hold still." A still bewildered Sam obliged. "Elsie is in Maine and can't see but that looks very not nice, anyway." She wiped the comic smear of lipstick from his mouth. Her body was calm as if nothing had happened. She thought as she cleaned his face, "I could no more go through with it than fly. Because I love Henry. Every bit of me belongs to him, every organ and nerve ending." She felt proud of her sudden frigidity. The liquor helped her forget the runaway moments.

"You said you'd help me," Ann said.

"Sure. One more kiss," Sam put his arms around her again. "You're irresistible."

"I want you to take me to the Café Madrid," she said. "Tonight. Now. I want to meet Liza King."

"Sure," Sam repeated. "Just one more."

How could a husband with a passionate wife like Elsie be so hungry for caresses? So starved—with starved hands and body? "My God—that's the way Henry was with Liza King," she thought, as a hand fumbled with her brassière. "The more sex I gave him the more exciting any stranger became."

She took advantage of a momentary delicacy on Sam's part, and stepped clear of him. "Yes," she thought, "an ounce of novelty is worth a pound of familiar pleasure."

"You're not sore?" Sam looked hungrily at her.

"No, why should I be? I enjoyed it as much as you did."

The statement seemed to bewilder Sam.

"You did?" he asked.

"Oh, yes," she smiled, "but we have to be a little sensible." She looked at him boldly. "Not all at once."

He stood gaping at her and giving off deep sighs.

"After what Henry's done to me, and to our marriage," she went on, "I'd be a fool to behave as if—as if I owed him anything."

"By God, you don't," said Sam, loyally.

"But it'll take me a little time to get used to the idea," she smiled, "at least a whole night. Sam, dear, will you take me somewhere—first?"

"Wait till I sit down a minute. I'm dizzy." He looked up at her tensely. "I want you to understand, I wasn't just making a pass. I've always been crazy about you. I've even confessed that to Elsie. If there was any woman other than her I'd go to bed with—it was you. And that's the truth, Ann. I'd rather hold you in my arms than any woman in the world—barring none. I've dreamed of it for eight years. It's a real love. I don't know what kind. But it's real. I'm just crazy about you. And when you kissed me, so help me God, I never felt anything in my life like it. Pure electricity."

She leaned over and kissed his cheek.

"I understand," she said. "I'm very grateful to you."

She sat on the arm of his chair and rumpled his thinning hair. "You're strong and reliable," she said. "Let's forget about us for the time being. Just a few hours."

"How can I?" Sam demanded. "I'm burning up. Oh, Ann, don't be so cruel."

She rose and poured him a drink. "Liza King first. I want to see her tonight." She smiled.

"Why?"

"Because she killed Sovey."

"Who did?"

"Liza King. That's why Henry's telling those lies. To protect her. I'm going to prove it. By tripping her up."

"Ann, you're mad. Just sit in my lap for a minute. We'll talk it over."

"Later. I've got to go upstairs and get ready," she said. "I'll be down in a minute."

"I'll go up with you," Sam rose, "and help you."

"No, Sam, please," she smiled. "I'll be right down and we'll make a night of it."

He sighed and nodded. "We've got lots of time," he said

as she went to the stairs. Ann realized that he had shrewdly added patience to his passion.

Fifteen minutes later, Sam was driving through the dark country night. Ann stared at the familiar road, a road that was almost part of her home. Tonight it was a road of desperate adventure that led to the Café Madrid and dangerous doings.

"You're about the most beautiful detective in the business," Sam grinned at her. His hand fell tentatively on her thigh.

Ann kept her leg motionless. She felt no tingle of response.

"I guess detectives are more moral than wives," she thought, and her heart beat exultantly at the prospect of Liza King and newspaper headlines proclaiming her arrest for murder.

The Café Madrid boasted of being among the most inhospitable and uncomfortable pleasure roosts in New York. Its tables were jammed against each other; its chairs provided only half a seat; its waiters were surly as a Georgia chain gang; its management treated customers as if they were a group of horrid misers; its food was mostly uneatable and the entertainment it offered was hardly a cut above imbecility. All these factors combined to make the Madrid the darling of the town's elite night idlers. In the absence of competition it was the audience who provided the show, the glamour, the importance of the Madrid—which is usually the secret of any great café's success.

Ann Lawrence sat entwined with her happy escort, there being no room for four legs and two bottoms at the tiny table to which they had been assigned by a "maître dee" who came out of his coma only at the sight of a twenty-dollar bill. A band was playing and a man and woman were stamping through a Spanish dance on the bit of floor reluctantly salvaged from the paying customers for a stage.

Sam ordered drinks and sandwiches.

"She comes on after this number," he tightened his grip on her knee. He slipped his other arm around her and squeezed her rib cage, loyally. "Heart's going like a trip hammer, isn't it?" he added.

It wasn't necessary to talk to Sam. He was too preoccupied with manual seduction to note any silence.

She remembered her first visit to the Madrid a week ago. It had been precipitated by a letter found in the lining of Henry's raincoat. Examining the coat to decide whether to throw it out or send it to the tailor's, she had come on an opened envelope, dated March 1, four months old. A short note inside begged Henry to forgive a "lonely, desperate Liza" for her filthy temper and to meet her at the Madrid, where she would be singing only for him at his usual table. "When you don't hold me in your arms for two days my knees get so weak I can hardly walk." There were some other anatomical bulletins.

It had been going on since March 1. A reanimated memory placed its beginning in early January. Henry's sudden devotion to his publishing business had developed with the New Year.

Two days after she found the letter, Henry had announced he was off on another three-day swing through the Middle West. And, asking for sympathy over the extra sales work he was doing, "Good-by, darling. Please miss me. I hate like the devil to go. But it's the only way to build up the business. The personal touch. Bookstores love a humble and mobile publisher." A long, deep kiss. An "I adore you, my sweet one." And he was off—to Liza. What a monster! That same night Ann had driven to the Café Madrid and watched her world collapse. She had stood, pale and staring, in the foyer. Liza King was singing. Alone, and ogling her from a ringside table, was the business builder Henry.

Tonight with Sam, the Madrid seemed a little less the Devil's anteroom than it had during that wretched half hour. Ann noticed that there was not as much original sin flourishing at its dimly lit tables as she had imagined then. The habitués were for the most part elderly, overbarbered men and sleek, bosomless girls in various stages of suspended animation. In fact, she and Sam seemed the only evidence of active libido in the place.

This was due to Sam, plus the seating deficiencies of the café. Jammed against her, he pawed away on her like a surreptitious xylophone player. Ann allowed these familiarities, and pretended even a flushed response, because they fitted into her project.

"Don't be so aloof," Sam breathed into her ear.

"I'm not being aloof," Ann smiled, and pressed her thigh against him by way of proof. "After all," she thought, "it's no worse than sitting in a crowded subway."

"Yes, you are," Sam sighed. "A man can tell."

"I'm having a delicious time," she said and moved her bare shoulder into his collar bone. The present phase of her project called for filling Sam with as much alcohol and amoral delusions as he could hold—without letting him get out of hand.

"That's my honey," Sam said. "Now I know you don't hate me."

"Do women ever hate you?" she laughed. "I don't believe it for a minute."

"You got me all wrong," Sam was offended. His words had thickened. "I'm not a woman chaser. Never even take one to lunch."

"Good lord," she thought, "he wants me to believe he's a good husband. As if there were two of him. He doesn't want me to lose sight of Elsie's devoted mate—while he pinches me black and blue."

Liza King would be certain to notice, particularly since all the other ringside males seemed in a coma. She wondered why this was and concluded that they had been sexually depleted by their light-o'-loves during the afternoon. Or, perhaps, sex didn't even figure among such men and women. "After men are old and impotent they keep advertising the fact that they are males by dozing publicly beside ornamental females." As for the ornamental females, Ann noted the skimpy calves, protruding neckbones and dried skin accompanying their fur, silks and jewels. "Dried up, sexless bean poles," she thought. "They belong more in a store window than in a bed."

Children were like that, able to live inside of pretenses. She remembered Henry—"Morality is chiefly a state of being angry at immorality. Since it's very difficult to be angry at oneself, one can never really be immoral. Only others can."

Sam's hand pressed harder. "I wonder if he works on Elsie in this fashion," she thought. As the pressure of his hand increased, she felt embarrassed. What he was doing looked so immoral, even if it meant nothing to her. "I mustn't wince like a frightened virgin," she thought, "or he'll notice. After all, I'm a woman of tremendous sexual experience." Eight years of bed acrobatics with Henry. "More sex probably than all these tootsies sitting here with their elderly keepers."

The lights on the tiny floor changed. A honking-voiced master of ceremonies flashed a set of artificial teeth in the spotlight and went into an announcement: "That lovely and glamorous artist of song, Miss Liza King. Let's give her a hand, folks. She's a real doll!"

A balloon-bosomed, wasp-waisted brunette materialized in the spotlight. Ann joined in the hand clapping.

"Now for God's sake," she warned herself. "No jealousy. I've got to see her as she is. Study her with Henry's eyes."

It was a difficult assignment. Jealousy kept spitting phrases and pictures into her head. "Very well," she thought, "he held her. Kissed her. Made love to her. Did all our

70

things with her. Even used the same words. But I must look
at her with my mind, not my bleeding heart. I've got to
solve her before I meet her. I have to make her friendly
toward me, if I expect her to confide in me."

Ann sipped her drink. There was one word for Liza—
voluptuous: a voluptuousness of manner more than body.
"Oh, she's built well enough," Ann thought, "a little too
strong boned for my taste. Almost horsey. But very voluptuous." The quality burned in the girl's damnably large blue
eyes and the wide, thick-lipped mouth. And the way she
held her head—like an animal strutting and sniffing. "She
acts as if she's a champion of something or other," Ann
frowned, "probably sex."

The flaring dark blue dress and its tight net bodice were
a trifle gauche. She bulged her clothes a bit too much. Ann
sighed. Her own body was a better one, but she wore it
inside her clothes. Liza was the kind of a strumpet whose
flesh seemed outside her clothes.

But there was no quibbling about the firm neck that
thrust itself out of them, and the exciting smile with which
Liza King greeted her audience—as if her lips were arms.
You had to grant her the gift of poise and command. But
there was something else. Just as a child on first look doesn't
seem like a child because it's too tall, Liza King seemed
unfeminine because there was too much of her. Not fat,
girth or height, but too much femaleness.

"I can't quite make her out," thought Ann. "She's strong
and arrogant. But there's something weak about her. Her
ankles are like mine. Small like her waist."

"That gal never murdered anybody," Sam whispered in her ear, "except between the sheets."

"Quiet, Sam, please," she said, and anchored his more active hand in hers. She thought, "No, I want her to see him pawing me." She released the hand and kissed Sam impulsively on his ear. A tender smirk filled his face and he turned his bloodshot eyes on her. "He's drooling," Ann thought. "If only he can remain like that."

Miss King began to sing of love and heartbreak. Her voice was husky and intimate, as if it came out of her partially exposed bosom rather than her larynx.

"A bedroom voice," Ann thought. "That's not really she. She's something else. She's invented that voice." An instinct warned Ann as the singing, like a vocal strip tease, filled the café. Liza was a vicious girl. "She's cruel and shrewd. I mustn't underrate her. She's uneducated. But full of cunning. Much keener than I am. More mystic, or something like that. It's not that she's more sexual herself, but that she knows how to make men more sexual.

"Her eyes are unreal," Ann added suddenly. "They're full of lies. She's mean, selfish and hates people."

Aloud, she said to Sam, "Quite beautiful, isn't she?"

"She looks like domestic stuff alongside you," said Sam.

"It's the dress," she said, "take that dress off and she's Venus."

"It's not that dress I'm dreaming of taking off," said Sam. He stroked her bare shoulders. "You're so beautiful, Ann, like a real altar."

72

"You're very sweet," Ann said. "Oh, Sam, I'd like to meet her."

She squeezed his knee and raised her face to him in a caricature of tenderness, lips atremble.

"I never felt like this in my life." Sam's voice was hoarse. "I don't care who's looking." He kissed her mouth and his body shook.

"Another Scotch for my friend," she smiled at the staring waiter.

"How about you, honey?" Sam asked.

"I don't dare take any more." Ann looked admiringly at him. "You're more than a match for me. I never saw a man hold his liquor like you."

"Make that a double Scotch," Sam said, and the waiter left.

❧

"Miss King will see you," the headwaiter smiled, twenty dollars' worth, and Ann stood up from the table. "I'm just drunk enough," she thought, "fuzzy but brilliant." Hadn't she been voted the "Girl Most Likely to Become Premier of France," in her senior year at Bennington? She giggled. Sam was following her through the café. A few of the oyster-faced roués turned from their benumbed blondes for a tired glance at her.

"I'm right behind you," said Sam, "all the way. Just call your shots, honey."

She smiled at Sam. He was very sweet. How much sweeter a man was intent on sin than on virtue. Apparently sin was a magic wand that evoked long-buried gallantry and youth.

They entered a narrow, crooked hall.

"The last door on the left," the headwaiter said.

Ann linked her arm with Sam's. He responded tenderly. "Did you ever hear the one about the husband who bought his wife a hair curler?"

"Save it," Ann patted his hand.

"I'm mad about you," Sam grew pensive and leaned. She kept him from falling over. "I got to hold you. You're so soft." He searched for a buttock.

Ann was pleased. There was one phase of life that Liza King must know well—the male rampant. There would be nothing phony about Sam Hartnett. He exuded gloat and seduction.

"The rest depends on me," she thought. As they walked, her arm guiding her pawing and sodden escort, she went swiftly over the hazards ahead. Liza could suspect her of only one aim, an underhanded wifely plot to pluck Henry out of her arms.

"She'll be looking for the Wives' Union Delegate to un-mask," Ann smiled. "She's probably had a lot of experience with wives going off like burglar alarms in her presence." Ann paused to straighten up Sam. "And she looks on wives as a pack of broken-down lunatics—without waistlines.

She's right. I hate wives, too. Elsie diddling around with her fishing tackle and a kerosene stove up in Maine. And wearing jeans, despite her broadened beam. And expecting Sam to turn into a eunuch in her absence."

She felt reassured. Her own contempt for wives would give her the right sound. It would blind the bosomy pirate to what Henry's wife was really up to.

"I must be careful not to seem interested in Sovey," she thought. "She killed him. She's buzzing with guilt. If I killed anyone, I'd be suspicious of anybody who looked at me sideways. Mustn't mention Sam Sovey. Or whatever his name was. Just let her talk. About Henry. If I disarm her completely she'll say things. Let them out. I know she will. She has a weak upper lip."

A voice called, "Come in," to Sam's knock.

"I don't get the logic," he whispered before opening the door, "but you just lead. I'll follow to hell and back."

Liza King was in a light gray suit. She was sitting on a kitchen chair in a small, perfume-reeking dressing room, and putting on her street shoes. She made no effort to hide her flamboyant legs.

"Hello," said Liza flatly. "So you're Henry's wife, eh? You want to sit down? Or do you fight standing up?"

"Thank you," said Ann. She sat down on a small couch. Sam squeezed into the space beside her.

"What do you want," Liza asked, "to do some hollering?"

"Not at all," Ann smiled. "I wanted to meet you—on an amiable basis."

"Don't talk like a jerk," Liza said coolly. "If you want

to holler, go ahead and get it over with. Only remember it's a hot night—and the windows are open."

"I wouldn't quite know what to holler about," Ann tried not to sound prissy. But her voice seemed artificial beside Liza's husky, direct tones. "Miss King, this is Mr. Hartnett."

Liza gave him a connoisseur's glance.

"How do you do," said Sam a little thickly. "Admired your singing."

"Sam loves music," Ann ruffled the back of his head with a gentle hand. Sam's response was perfect. His mouth hung open, his eyes rolled up and he muttered lovingly, "Don't do that, honey. I'm crazy for you." She patted his hand, and Sam remained inert and concupiscent.

"I'll be God damned," said Liza. "I noticed you two out front." The shoes were on. "What's this all about? If you don't want to holler, what do you want?"

"I wanted to talk to you about Henry. I felt perhaps between us we could clear things up."

"Such as—?" Liza King became a cocked pistol. Ann thought, "She really despises me. Maybe on account of Sam." She turned to him. "Have you a cigarette, darling?"

"Anything you want, honey." With rubber fingers, Sam fished a package out of a pocket. He helped her light it, singeing her nose. "You're adorable," he hiccoughed, "Queen of Carthage."

"Thank you, sweet." Ann looked at his hand protectively on her kneecap. She smiled at an expressionless Liza and added, "Henry's all alone. We haven't been very close. Poor Henry. And I don't know how to speak to him any more—

76

to give him any comfort. And I hate thinking of him alone—in his great trouble. That's why I'm here. Sam insisted I see you. Didn't you, darling?" She patted the protecting hand.

"Absolutely," Sam's voice wobbled. "All the time."

"What do you mean you're not very close?" The pistol remained cocked and the siren's neck stiffened.

"Hasn't he told you?" Ann asked.

"He's told me plenty." Liza bared a set of necklacey teeth. She was possibly smiling; Ann couldn't tell. "But I got a habit of not believing what men tell me. Especially husbands with their coat collars up like Commie spies."

"She hates him," Ann thought, "or maybe she wants him too much."

"Yes," she smiled at Liza King, "Henry's quite a liar when he puts his mind to it. But I don't think he's lied to you!"

"No?" Liza was grim with reminiscence.

Ann noted the quick temper that hit her face like a storm. It went with her high insteps and arched neck. But there was something odd about her temper—as if it were shallow. And that querulous upper lip. Henry had said long ago, "A woman's lower lip is for kissing. The upper one for crying. Watch out for an upper lip that looks overused."

"I mean, I can't imagine what Henry could have to lie to you about." She smiled at the violent face. "That is, as far as I'm concerned. My God," she beamed suddenly, "he hasn't got *another* girl, has he?"

"Talkin' about Henry?" Sam inquired. "My best friend. Went to school together. Brilliant. But nothin' solid."

"Quiet, Sam." Ann ruffled his back hair and Henry's best friend looked throbbingly at her.

"The reason I imagine Henry hasn't lied to you—much," Ann resumed, "is because he hasn't had any reason to. We haven't meant much to each other for some time. We were once deeply in love, of course. I hope he hasn't denied that. Oh, madly in love. But there's nothing as fatal to real love as a long dose of marriage." She remembered one of Henry's lines: "Sex is a feast that marriage turns into a midnight snack." She watched Liza's face as she fished for other probable Henry speeches to her harem rival. The widening of the blue eyes told her she had struck Henry-gold. "Of course," she went on, "it usually doesn't matter in a marriage if love dies. Marriages are kept going like lodges. You don't have to attend any meetings. Just pay your dues and write a letter once in a while—and you stay a life member."

"You trying to tell me," Liza interrupted, "there's nothing personal between you and Henry?"

"Oh, we have a certain fondness for each other," Ann sighed. "I send out his laundry. And we preserve a social front."

"When did he last go to bed with you?" Liza's eyes blazed at her.

"Unfair question," Ann smiled. "Two people living in the same house. Accidents are bound to happen." Liza's eyes were guiding her. "But—we've been accident free for three months."

"Well, I'll be damned," said Liza. "You talk just like him." She stared at Ann, a stare as shameless as a child's.

78

"I haven't been as lucky as you," she said. "It's been just one continuous round of 'accidents.'"

Ann's belly contracted as if someone had punched it, but she kept her smile intact. "What a monster," she thought. The monster was Henry. "Only four nights ago. Swooning with passion. His cover-up. That's why he's been so damned sexual with me. To lull my suspicions. And salve his conscience at the same time. But how could he do it—with her on his agenda?" She stared back at Liza and thought, "She must be a fake. Her sex all on the outside."

Sam was talking, his words running more and more together. He thought it was time for a drink all around. He would send out for champagne.

"Butt out, Junior," Liza King frowned at him. "You've had enough. Close your eyes and go to sleep."

"You're the domineering type," Sam said. "Nothing soft about you. No Queen of Carthage."

"Be a good boy," Ann patted his cheek. "You've had quite enough to drink—darling."

"If you say so," Sam said. "Because I'm crazy about you." He stared mystically at her feet. "I'd like to help you put on your stockings," he moaned, "if you please."

Ann smiled at the attentive Liza. "He's very sweet. And gentle. Quite the opposite of Henry."

"Yes, he must seem very boyish," said Liza, "after Dracula."

"Henry?" Ann smiled. "Poor Henry."

"A few days in jail won't hurt him."

"I wasn't thinking of his present troubles," said Ann.

"You see, I know him so well. He must have felt awful when you didn't believe him. I mean, when you thought he was lying about his marriage meaning nothing to him. It hasn't really, for some years."

"Barring accidents," said Liza.

"Oh, there weren't many," Ann smiled. "Please forgive me."

Liza laughed loudly. It was a laugh full of vitality and it showed her plump tongue and the mysterious roof of her mouth.

"You're a knockout," Liza said. "I'm on the ropes, so help me." She grinned and Ann envied her flash of teeth. "When I heard you wanted to see me, I got ready for a real rough-and-tumble. I thought you'd come in here all ooglie-booglie and I was going to sock you, so help me, the minute you got out of order."

"Ooglie-booglie?" Ann smiled.

"I mean nuts. You know how wives are," Liza chuckled, "always shooting down poachers. So you wanted to find out if I have any real feeling for Henry—and if I'll help him and stick to him. Right?"

"Yes," said Ann. "I feel a certain loyalty—but I'm sort of out of the picture."

"Yes, I love Henry." Liza looked dourly at her guest. "He's a horrible bastard in lots of ways."

"I know," Ann said.

"He's made me more miserable than any two men I've ever known. Was he always such a sarcastic sadist?"

"More or less," Ann said, "after he's had you." She blushed slightly.

"I can't stand sarcasm," Liza said. "That's even worse than a liar." She paused. "And now he gets into this pot of trouble with Sovey."

"I *do* hope he's telling the police the truth—that he never met the poor man." Ann flashed her suburbia smile.

"I hope so, too," Liza said. Ann heard the lie in her tone and tried to look abstracted. "How can a bright man like Henry be so stupid?" Liza said. "I told him Tom Sovey hadn't laid a finger on me for eight months. And I mean that. I'm telling you, I've been true to that godam Henry—while he was having his little accidents with you." She stared at Ann. "Imagine living with that mongoose for eight years without going nuts. He's quite a novelty. Even for a girl like me."

"You seem a very nice girl," said Ann.

"Do I really?" Liza smiled. "I'm glad you approve of me."

"I wasn't being sarcastic," said Ann. "I never am."

Liza looked at her intently. "I love Henry," she said, "like mad. And he loves me the same way. I don't want you to have any other impression."

"I haven't," Ann said, and tried to keep the pain in her heart from pumping dolor into her voice. "And I'm glad you're honest. Because if you love him, Liza, that's all that matters. He's got someone. *I* couldn't help him if I tried."

"Look, kid," Liza smiled. "I'm hungry. I usually have my supper after the show."

"Can't we go some place cozy?" Ann said. "Do you know the Organdy Room?"

"I've forgotten what a real restaurant looks like," said Liza. "I've been hiding out in basement spaghetti joints with your godam husband."

"We'll go," said Ann. "Sam!" She shook her half-comatose escort.

"We can't bring him into a restaurant," Liza stood up. "Come on, what's good enough for Henry's good enough for his wife. We'll go to my joint and I'll cook up some frozen stuff."

"I'll help you!" Ann beamed. Sam rose with difficulty.

"Can't you ditch him?" Liza asked.

"Oh, honey, that wouldn't be fair." Ann smiled at the weaving Sam. "He'll be all right. He never gets noisy." She searched her college days for a proper phrasing. "He's a real dream-boat."

"I can't keep this up," thought Ann, filling her plate with macaroni. Her betrayed wifehood was back in her heart. The Henry crime was new again, happening for the first time again. "I'm going to scream and start blubbering. The rotten man. Rotten, rotten from head to foot!"

She controlled herself and ate prettily.

Against the wall a few yards from her plate was an oversized bed covered with a red velvet quilt. Sam was lying on it, grunting in a torpor. On the wall were a dozen framed photographs, eight of them of Liza King and four of Henry Lawrence. Two of the Henry pictures were inscribed: To MY SKYROCKET LIZA, HER LOVING HENRY, and TO LIZA, MY ANACONDA—FROM HER MORSEL, HENRY.

Ann was unaware of the rest of the large studio room. The wall, bristling with photographs of Liza's anatomical high points; and the bed—the awful arena of unfaithful lust—held all her senses captive. She could neither see nor think beyond them.

"I don't for a minute believe he killed that poor Tom Sovey," Liza spoke as she ate.

"You don't, really?"

"No," Liza's eyes stared into hers. "Do you?"

"Of course not."

She returned Liza's prying stare until Liza lowered her eyes. "She's acting," Ann thought, "fooling me, and being cautious."

"I was so godam mad at Henry that night," Liza said, "that I was glad to hear he'd been arrested for something the next day. Even murder. My God, what a bastard he can be."

"He can be that," said Ann thoughtfully.

"We'd had this fight," Liza went on. "About Tom Sovey. Poor Tom was broke and wanted a loan. He was pleading with me on the phone. And Henry insists he's making a pass at me, and I'm encouraging him. And that isn't all. He says he has proof I've been sleeping with Tom. God, I could have killed him. I mean, Henry."

"I know. He can be very trying," Ann sighed, "but I don't understand why he should shoot your friend Tom."

"I don't think he shot him," said Liza. The blue eyes stared again. Ann smiled into them, "I mean, why should the police think he did?"

"Jealousy," said Liza. "They've probably talked to people who heard him carrying on with me."

"In public?" Ann widened her eyes.

"In public. In private. In bed. In a taxi. Any damn place," said Liza, "the most horribly jealous idiot I've ever known. And always over nothing."

"Well," Ann said, "that's quite a new side of him." She tried a lewd smile. "He never seemed to mind my giving it away."

"The sonofabitch told me you were true blue."

"I was for a time. A short time," Ann sighed. "But he made life too impossible."

"That's not the first one?" Liza glanced at the dormant Sam.

"Hardly," said Ann.

Liza scowled, "I was absolutely faithful to him. And he kept howling at me. He was even jealous of Tony, the head-waiter. And of my sawed-off agent. He even made me cut out my movie-star number—because I showed too much."

"I can't help feeling a bit depressed by all this," Ann said. "He always had quite the opposite attitude about me.

Even on our honeymoon. He loved me to parade around Miami in a Bikini."

"He's psychopathic both ways," said Liza.

"Did he have a gun on him when he left you that night?" Ann asked, casually.

"A gun? Henry?" Liza laughed. "He'd just as soon carry a bow and arrow. He hated guns."

"I never knew that."

"He kept insisting I get rid of mine," Liza nodded. "I keep it on the floor, under the bed. An old habit. Henry hated it because he said it inhibited him. He couldn't be as nasty as he wanted—with a gun on the premises."

"I can't imagine your owning a gun," Ann said.

"An ex-sweetie gave it to me for Christmas."

"An odd gift," Ann said.

"He was a policeman," Liza sighed. "Wait a minute!" She stared. "I hope it's still there."

"What?" Ann's heart beat with excitement.

"My gun," Liza left the table. She knelt and reached under the bed. "I keep it right in front, at the head." She continued feeling the floor with her hand. "I'll be damned. It's gone." She stood up. "I'll get a light." Ann watched her walk to the kitchen and return with a flashlight and go to her knees again. The illumined floor under the bed was empty of pistols.

"I'll be damned," Liza frowned. "Somebody has taken it."

"Maybe your cleaning woman." Ann was in her chair again. She felt exultant. "That's the trick," she thought. "They'll find her gun and she'll pretend Henry stole it."

"I'm going to notify the police first thing in the morning," said Liza. "I don't want my gun turning up as the murder weapon. And leave me holding the bag."

Ann thought, "She's really scared. Or maybe she's just acting for me." Her thought stopped and a memory came to her that dizzied her for an instant.

"What is it?" Liza asked.

"Nothing," Ann said.

"You turned pale," Liza said.

Ann thought, "I'd better tell her. Or she'll lose faith in me." Aloud she said, "I just remembered something. About Henry."

"What?" Liza's neck straightened.

Ann thought, "I mustn't lie." She sighed and said, "The night of the murder. I came home late, you know. I'd been out with Sam. When I entered the hall I heard Henry on the phone talking to you. I blew him a kiss and went upstairs, but I couldn't help hearing part of what he said to you. Only when the police came for him in the morning, I forgot it. I told Sam tonight if I could only remember it, it would prove Henry was innocent. And I remember it now."

Ann moved from the table to a large stuffed chair.

"What do you remember?" Liza watched her.

"He was saying, as I came in," said Ann, " 'Hello, my Liza sweet, I just wanted to tell you how sorry I am about Tom. But I'm pretty sure he won't pester you again. Ever!' That's all I heard."

"You're a truthful kid," Liza said quietly. "Those are the exact words. That's what's kept me worrying since the cops told me about Sovey." She looked at Ann with large furtive eyes. Ann thought, "She lies like a frightened child."

"It sounds pretty cold-blooded, killing Tom and calling me up and cooing that Tom wouldn't ever pester me again," Liza looked away. "If I was as transparent as she is," Ann thought, "Henry would whoop with laughter. She's utterly stupid—as an actress."

"I wish somebody hadn't copped that pistol," said Liza.

"Oh, it'll turn up," Ann said casually. She smiled, "I know why I had that stoppage about his phone call. Because it made him sound guilty. Even if it didn't mean he killed Sovey it means he saw him. And is lying about something."

"And you remembered when you heard my gun was missing," said Liza.

"That's right. The mind's an odd contraption. You didn't tell the police about Henry's call, did you?"

"No," said Liza.

Ann felt excitement. Liza had finally lied to her about something. She *had* told Sergeant Davies about the phone call.

"May I use your bathroom?"

Liza pointed to a door and remained motionless.

In the bathroom, Ann thought about several things at once. First, about the inscribed photographs on the wall. "I knew, I knew," she insisted. But the inscribed photographs were more than knowing—the wifely "knowing" which is always hopeful that it will be deceived out of existence. The love-inscribed photographs were indelible

87

confessions that could never be lied away. They said that her Henry had transferred himself into another world, moved his heart into an alien terrain. And the alien terrain, this erotic lithograph of a woman, belonged body, grin and temper to Henry, now sitting in jail. "If not for that, he'd be lying stretched in that bed of hers," she thought.

Liza's words echoed in her mind.

"She's full of lies about everything. About Henry, Sovey, herself," Ann thought, "and about that missing gun. Maybe there never was a gun, and she's just pulling my leg. But why? To mix me up. That's what she'd do if she's guilty. But if Sovey was trying to blackmail Henry, why should she kill the man? To protect Henry from my finding out? Hardly. She'd more likely join Sovey in his threats to expose Henry. In her own way, she was probably blackmailing him, too. Threatening to leave him if he didn't walk out on me."

As she thought these and other quick things, Ann washed her hands in the basin and looked eagerly around. A bathroom was a place for clues. Towels or rags that had wiped up bloodstains. A laundry bag hung in a corner. It was half filled. Ann rummaged through crumpled linen and lingerie. No bloodstains. But in the pocket of a coffee-stained bed jacket there was a letter. That seemed to be her forte as a detective, Ann thought, finding incriminating letters. She removed the opened envelope. It was Hotel San Mareno stationery. The name Thomas Sovey was scrawled on the back flap as part of the return address. Inside the envelope were some twenty bits of paper. Liza had torn up Sovey's letter intending to flush it down the toilet. But had forgotten. The envelope was dated five days ago.

Ann concealed the find under her skirt belt. She would put the pieces together and read them when she got home. She must get home quickly, now. Liza's voice called, "You all right?"

"Oh, yes." She must have been in the bathroom quite a while. She closed the laundry bag. Liza had been having coffee in bed, viz the coffee-stained bed jacket. She had read the morning mail. Furious or frightened by the Sovey letter, she'd torn it up, intending disposal. She might remember it now, and look in the laundry bag. And become suspicious if the letter were gone.

Ann came out of the bathroom.

"Sit down," said Liza, "you look beat up."

"Too much liquor," said Ann. "That Sam. Always leads me astray." There were no suspicions in Liza's face. A preoccupied, deep stare. Ann sat down.

"I've been thinking," said Liza, "Mr. Henry Lawrence didn't shoot Tom. That phone call proves it."

"It does?"

"Absolutely. I know Henry's voice. I know all his putonski mannerisms. He was sincerely happy when he called me—and Henry couldn't be happy—over a murder."

Ann tried not to react to the bold, shifty eyes that called the words lies, or to the insincere enthusiasm, the fake comradeliness of the liar.

"She's trying to figure out something to make Henry seem innocent," Ann thought. "Because she knows he is. She

89

knows he's sitting in jail because he won't tell something damning about her. So she's sort of repaying him. But for me to notice. Not the police."

"You're right," Liza said. "I ought to visit my gentleman friend. It's so absolutely silly—his sitting in jail. There's no case against him. I can't understand the police being so extra stupid."

Ann thought, "I'll know more about how stupid they are when I read that letter. She's sorry Henry's in trouble over her. But not sorry enough to do anything about it."

Liza went to a sideboard that held liquor bottles. Ann noted a change in her. Tension seemed to go out of her movement and her outlines seemed to soften. A glow of friendliness was in the vividly blue eyes.

"I feel better about the whole messy business," Liza smiled. "Cheer up, beauty."

Beauty! Ann hid a nervousness behind her suburbia smile, and forgot about the torn letter tucked in her belt. Liza brought a drink to her.

"Here, we'll drink together," Liza held up her glass. "To our friend Henry." Ann drank with her.

"You're much prettier than I imagined," said Liza. Her shining eyes looked boldly at Ann. Her voice became gentle.

Sitting on the arm of the chair, Liza said, "It's no fun losing a man like Henry. And having to settle for guys like that." She indicated the sleeping Sam. "I know how it is. I once lost a man. A gentleman cop. We were going to get married. Only I caught him cheating once too often. I gave him his whistle and told him to blow. It hurt like hell. Other

90

guys made it worse. Guys like Tom Sovey. Henry took the
pain away, finally. By handing me another pain. They're
all good for only one thing—to torture you. That's the way
you know you're in love with a man—if he can turn the
screws on you and pull you out of shape."

Her hand touched Ann's shoulder gently.

"You're very lovely," Liza said. "You've got that rose petal
kind of skin. Poor Ann."

Liza's head pressed slightly against hers and Ann sat
bewildered and silent. It was almost as if Henry were speaking to her. The same soft and knowing voice that seemed
to be inside her senses. The hand was back on her shoulder.
It moved slightly over her bared back and slowly down her
arm.

"I envy your shoulders," Liza said. "I bet Henry never
called *you* the All-American halfback. But we have the
same arms. Except yours are softer to touch." Her fingers
squeezed the triceps. "No muscles," she smiled.

Ann said nothing. She thought of the torn letter under
her belt, but the thought slipped away. An alertness that
had nothing to do with detection filled her. Liza was wooing
her. Radiating hints, hopes, whispers, and becoming startling
and near. She remembered how Sam had pawed her for
several hours. Except for the first moments of their kissing,
she had felt no sensation other than acting triumph.

Now her skin shivered. She was afraid to speak or move.
She could feel Liza's troubled eyes watching her like a child,
begging for something. Ann's mind became blank. She sat
without thought while rivulets of sensation ran through her.

91

The pause was too long, the silence too obvious. Ann looked up. The blue eyes watching her, waited. There was no hiding from their open look, no acting for them.

Ann's thought was back. "I shouldn't have stayed silent so long. She's queer. She's a Lesbian. My God, it can't be! But she is. She's loving me with her eyes and hands and silence. I can feel it."

The last four words startled her.

"I've got to get Sam home," she said aloud.

"He's doing all right," Liza said. "Shame to disturb the Sleeping Beauty."

Ann stood up. Her skin tingled with caress echoes. "I must be exhausted," she thought. There was a weakness in her knees that made her almost sit down again—in the same chair.

"No, I've got to get him to his home," she smiled, "in case his wife calls up. She's in Maine, fishing."

Ann shook Sam's shoulder. Sam sat up abruptly. His movements were steady but his mind was absent.

"We're going home," Ann said. Sam nodded. He wanted a cigarette in dumb show. She found and lit one and put it between his lips. Liza was watching, still sitting on the arm of the chair her guest had occupied.

"I'm glad you're convinced Henry's innocent," Ann said, "because if he weren't, I'm sure you'd be the first to know it. And I hope you can cheer him up while he has to squat in that horrid jail. Poor Henry. Thanks, anyway, for cheering me up. I'm glad to know you." Fear was in her, as if the room had become full of danger. The inscribed photographs, the obvious Liza lies, the torn letter from Sovey were part of the danger. But there was more to it.

"She's lying. She's lying!" Ann's mind whispered desperately. She held onto Sam's arm as she opened the hall door. The lies were like the roar of a brass band. She had never seen so quickly, deeply, into another human, except once.

"Good night," said Ann, "and thank you for the supper. We'll see each other again."

Liza remained silent. Moving quickly into the hall, Ann knew without looking back that Liza with the gentle hands and brass band lies was sitting on the empty chair arm and watching her with large, beggar's eyes.

Sam remained aloof during the drive along the Hudson River. Ann forgot to think about him. There were no thoughts of Henry or of the murder clues or of Liza King in her mind. She drove through the dark, tree-tunneled road along the river with only the present in her consciousness. The present was an empty, curving road leading ultimately to Englewood. She raced over its familiar turns and admired the dark face of the river and the doll's house lights twinkling on its far bank, as if she were a tourist come on a new romantic scene.

"The river's like a long, dark snake," Ann thought. She

shivered at this simile and thought, "She wrote lovely poetry." She was thinking of her college roommate Margo—the one human in her life into whom she had looked deeply. Liza brought the Margo memories back. She didn't bother to think why. "Funny that we never corresponded. We were going to write every month of our lives. Exchange secrets every month. And not a word. She's probably married now, with children."

Henry hadn't wanted any child for them—not yet. "We'll become parents after we've got nothing better to be," he said in the beginning. "Let's say in five years." He had postponed parenthood another five years when the time came. He said, "Children are an interruption. They interrupt the hell out of life, love, ego. That's why there's so much child hatred in the world. The longer we wait, the less trouble children can make us—the less to interrupt." And they were still waiting. Why all this thinking about children? Liza was the answer. Her begging child's eyes.

Ann slowed down in the town. She considered the best way of getting Sam into his house without reviving his enthusiasm for her. When the car stopped in front of the Hartnett Tudor house, Sam's wits automatically returned.

"Where are we?" he asked.

"Home," she said. "Have you got your key?"

"My key?" Sam was petulant. "Let's go to your place."

"It's terribly late, Sam."

He held a key in his hand. They walked up the veranda steps. Sam unlocked the door.

"Good night," Ann said. He pulled her into the vestibule.

"Mad about you," he said. He looked at her with confused eyes. "Elsie's bed," he said hoarsely, and staggered away from her. She watched him weave into the living room and collapse on a couch. His head hung corpselike over its side. Entering the room, she lifted his legs onto the couch and put a pillow under his head. His face was smeared with lipstick. She feared waking him up if she tried to remove it.

She walked out of the house. The street was bare with night. Walking the tree-arcaded blocks to her home, she remembered a poem of Margo's: "The night tiptoes around us, the dark trees are like fingers raised for silence."

In her bed an hour later, Ann's mind became a noisy auditorium full of many speakers. Liza's voice was the most insistent, Margo's voice was almost its twin in sound. And Margo had been her best friend, her only real friend before Henry. She remembered Margo's large, dark eyes, different from Liza's, but with the same childlike gift of intimacy in them. She remembered Liza's straight neck and the touch of her hands and thought, "She's not a real Lesbian, but one of those women with a castration complex."

She smiled because Margo's voice was talking now. She could hear its special husky tones, its witty inflections. It was much different from Liza's voice. She had forgotten its special quality. How could one forget a voice that had meant so much. All those all-night talks in their dark dormitory. For two or three years. Inseparable. Even during summer vacations. Because Margo, with all her genius, was a child. Left alone, without guidance, she was certain to get run over by a streetcar or fall into a creek.

Liza was a crude caricature of Margo, she frowned. Not even that. There was nothing in common, except how she, Ann, felt toward them. They were the only two transparent humans she had ever known. You could look into Margo as you could into a goldfish bowl and see all her bright thoughts swimming around.

"There are women who aren't actually Lesbian but who feel that they were castrated at birth, or just before birth, by some trick of fate. Or by their parents' mismanagement." Margo spoke again in Ann's mind—each inflection intact as if the voice had been preserved on a record. Margo knew so much. She read all the books. And had thousands of thoughts and theories. How stupid to have broken the friendship. It was Henry's fault. She had started to tell him about Margo. He misunderstood everything. "Sounds like a typical case of puppy love Lesbianism," Henry beamed. "Allow me to plagiarize from George Moore's *Story-Teller's Holiday*. A village character listening to a tale of amour cries out, 'skip all that stuff, m'boyo, and begin with the boobies.'" That ended Margo as a conversation piece. She'd have told gladly, if there'd been anything to tell. There was less to confess than about Liza tonight.

Ann shuddered pleasantly, "How could a murderess get so tender and cloying?" Her thought drifted sleepily between past and present. The image persisted of Liza sitting, bending under the bed, moving across the room; of Liza's eyes begging, of her delicately touching fingers and the swell of her bosom and of the sharp, sweet odor of her hair close to her. She wondered if Margo's description of a certain type of modern woman fitted Liza. Women who wanted to be men but were actually infants. "They spend their lives in a sort of mystic quest of the male organ," Margo said, "and they usually despise their female side and try to soil it by giving themselves to man after man. The percentage of suicides is very high among them."

And how did Margo know? From reading books, of course. They had both been too innocent to know anything, except as readers.

The dark dormitory with its moonlit windows and the youthful reach of two adolescents for all the unknown things came into Ann's mind. She lay in the lumpy college bed again, and smiled. "It's very complicated," she said, as if enjoying a jest. "Liza can't be like that. She's mad about Henry." She listened to Margo explain that oddity, "Those kind of women often get madly attached to a man, not to love him but to imitate him. They become a sort of phantom male that way."

Ann hoped she was falling asleep. But sleep disappeared. Today and long ago seemed mysteriously embraced. Was it Liza who was the castration-complex type? Or herself, Ann? Good lord, not herself! There had never been anything, not a furtive thought or an erotic daydream, between her and Margo. Nothing had entered their comradeship—except words. It couldn't be herself, Ann thought. She had been exposed to a woman, younger, lovelier and more charming than Liza, and no sex had ever touched her nerves. No hint of sex. No surreptitious caresses. No secret phantasies in her lonely hours.

"Almost too innocent," she thought, "but then, I was completely innocent." She tried to remember her early sex sensations. There hadn't been any—until Henry. She'd never necked with boys. "You have to start sometime, I know, Margo. But I can't stand them. Grabbing you in cars and on verandas. Like bats jumping into your hair."

Then Henry had materialized on a boat riding to London. No bat, Henry. But a wondrous talker. Like Margo. Henry was touring Europe, drumming up new authors for his publishing firm. Book talk had come first. He had hired her after two weeks as a reader and translator. She was full of college French and Italian. Then people talk, psychology talk. Religion, anthropology, taboos. And thus to sex inquiry. Verbal. A whole month without any caressing tries. That's how she fell in love—listening. By the time he took her in his arms, she was already in love, dependent on his talk for excitement. Dolorous when his voice was elsewhere.

Then four months of living together "in sin." Ann shuddered at the sin-memory. Because there had been none. No sin. No sensation. She had remained frigid, wanton, eager, obliging and miserably incompetent. As if someone had forgotten to equip her.

Henry had noticed quickly and been kind and knowing. He continued their sexual bouts as if they were laboratory experiments. Until one night! The night had always been a red-letter night to remember. She was standing nude in the Miami hotel bedroom waiting for Henry. He came into the room, smiled at her, embraced her standing up. As he was starting his hundredth experiment, Ann happened to

98

look over her shoulder. She saw herself naked in a door mirror. The sight of the naked woman in the mirror changed her life. She screamed with passion, as Henry held her. They were married two weeks later.

Ann sat up suddenly. The name Liza seemed to fill the room. "Good lord, I must have fallen asleep without knowing it. I was dreaming. The letter. Sovey's letter!" She was out of bed. The envelope lay on the floor where it had fallen when she was undressing.

She took the pieces to her small desk. Two pages had been torn into eighths. Liza had strong fingers. "I used to be good at jigsaw puzzles," she thought. It took an hour. She sat rereading the reassembled letter pasted on two sheets of her own stationery.

Dear Liza:
  Please don't try to be too smart. I've limped along like a run-over dog—too long. My limp is gone. Also I have a new type of brain. I advise you to take note of it. A brain that's tired of squeaking apologies. I need money, Liza. You owe me that much, at least. After all you've taken from me. I need money viciously, and you'll give it to me. One hundred dollars a week—beginning Monday. If not, I file suit against you for divorce and I name that literary dandy of yours, Mr. Lawrence, as your lover and my home-wrecker. It'll make juicy copy for the less esthetic journals. I may also decide to add the Princess to our court proceedings. Oh, what a fascinating side show that would be

for the gutter trade. One hundred dollars per week and I shall be content to remain your negligible and invisible husband for as long as the ghost walks.

Yours dutifully,

Tom

P.S. I'll be waiting at this address to hear from you Monday evening.

T.S.

Solving a crime was so easy, Ann thought. She stood up drowsily. "Poor Liza," she sighed, and went back to her bed.

Bright morning lighted the room. Hannah shuffled in with the breakfast tray and the morning papers. Ann said, "Good morning, dear Hannah. I haven't slept a wink. I'm completely exhausted."

"That husband's goin' to be all right, dear modom," Hannah croaked. "Nice pictures of everybody in all the papers."

Ann thought, "I'd better call Sam and hand over Sovey's letter to him." She saw Liza behind the wire mesh in Henry's place. "I feel almost as upset about turning her over to the police as Henry did. But not quite as much." She smiled suburbia's smile. "I'll tell Sam after lunch." She laughed. She was keeping Henry in jail a half-day longer—on purpose. "And I'll tell him so, too!"

Sitting up in bed, Ann looked through the papers. Large photographs of herself and Liza King smiled out of their columns. Liza's smile was the flashier. Henry's face was also on display, but it was of smaller mold, and seemed less familiar to her than Liza's boldly beaming features.

"Missus Hartnitt's downstairs," Hannah re-entered, "and she's comin' up."

"Elsie!" Ann put the papers away. "Good lord, when did *you* get back?" She smiled at the plumpish figure and creamy face in the doorway. "Come in, darling. The last person I expected to see!"

"My dear, sweet Ann," Elsie pulsated to the bed. The friends embraced. "I had to come back," Elsie said. A small gurgle of grief disturbed her suburbia tones. "I couldn't stay away, Ann, with you in this horrible situation. Ghastly. Utterly ghastly."

"It's clearing up," Ann began. "I've found some evidence—"

"Oh, Ann, Ann," Elsie's refined face quivered with woe. "Those men! Those human pigs always heading for the slime! They're all alike. Cruel, dirty, lying things!"

Tears filled Elsie's pale eyes. The aristocratic nose turned pink and Elsie began to sob.

"Good lord," Ann thought, "it's Sam. Sam's done something." She swallowed nervously. She knew what it was.

"I came home an hour ago," Elsie said. "I took one of those wretched local planes. A dreadful flight. But I knew you needed me, poor Ann. You're closer to me than anyone in the world. I just couldn't bear to think of you in Engle-

101

wood alone. And, oh, Ann!" her head moved from side to side in torment, "I found Sam asleep on the library couch, his neck, ears, mouth smeared with lipstick!"

Ann controlled what would have been a hysterical laugh.

"That ungrateful pig," said Elsie, "to take advantage of me after the way I forgave him last time. After that little Vassar pervert. You remember how he moaned and pleaded and said he'd kill himself if I didn't give him another chance. And I gave the wretched man another chance. And what happens? What do I get for it? The minute I'm out of Englewood he's off after another cheap, vulgar pervert."

"What did Sam say?" Ann asked.

"Oh, the usual lies and howls," Elsie said. "That he was drunk. Out with some men. Some hussy came to their table and started pawing him. He can't even remember what she looked like."

"It might be true," said Ann.

"Lies! Lies!" Elsie cried. "I can always tell when he's lying. He gets a cringe in his voice. And starts blubbering. I loathe him. I'll never let him touch me again. Ann, please don't stick up for him. I know about Henry and that girl. And it's the same with Sam."

"I wouldn't stick up for him for a minute," said Ann. "Men are all brutes and liars!"

"Filthy animals," said Elsie, at the end of her sobbing. Ann wondered at the absence of guilt in her, as well as gallantry. She felt no qualms about Sam being punished alone for his sins. As for involving herself by explaining the whole thing to Elsie, that was unthinkable. "She'd never believe it was innocent," Ann thought, and blushed unexpectedly. If Sam hadn't stopped to set down his highball glass—it would have been a moot point as to who raped whom.

"Oh, thank you, darling," Elsie was burbling. "Do you mind if I stay here? I'll use the guest room. I don't want to be anywhere Sam can get at me. He has the keys to all our bedrooms. I'd simply die if he ever touched me again."

"Of course you may stay," Ann squeezed her friend's soft hand, and thought, "My character's going all to hell. I ought to feel sorry for her. But damn it, she isn't entitled to any sympathy. Even if she were in the right, which she isn't." She paused. The image of Liza flared in her mind. That's the way Liza must have thought of her—a wife who can't hold her husband faithful has no claim on his fidelity— or on anyone's compassion.

"Oh, my God!" Elsie cried. "You dare come here! Into my haven! Get out, you whoremonger!"

Ann stared at Sam in the doorway. He was freshly shaved and looked pink but no longer rouged. Elsie's rage increased at his silence.

"If you move one step nearer me, I'll jump out of that window, so help me God! You horrible, loathsome tramp lover."

Sam spoke in a dignified voice. "I'm Henry's lawyer. My best friend's life is at stake. And I need a clear head, my dear. I ask you, Elsie, to help me—for Henry's sake."

"Get out!" Elsie screamed. "Don't you dare come in here."

"Please, Elsie, darling—believe me. I've told you the absolute God's own truth. I'm innocent."

"You whoremonger," Elsie moaned. "Behind my back! You never change. The minute my back's turned you turn into a beast. And go after your perverts!"

"Elsie, I swear to God, I'm innocent," Sam moaned. The dignity was out of his voice. "Darling, let's not make a scene in front of poor Ann. She has her own problems."

"You're worse than Henry Lawrence by a thousand times," Elsie screamed. "I can't bear to look at you. Betraying me! With some filthy little whore! After all I've given you. My love. My honor. My virtue. I want to die!"

Tears came from Sam's eyes. Elsie rushed, blinded with a louder grief, into the bathroom. The phone rang.

"It's a Miss King for you, Mis' Ann," Hannah looked into the room.

"I'll take it downstairs," Ann got out of bed. Sam stared mournfully at her rumpled nightgown.

"Don't tell Elsie," he whispered. "I can't bear her suffering."

"There's nothing to tell, you idiot," she said.

"Not so loud," Sam whispered, "she has ears like a snake." He wiped his eyes. "For God's sake, don't give me away."

Ann put on a robe. "Of course not, you utter fool!"

"We weren't together at all last night," Sam's whisper followed her into the hall. She slammed the door on the bathroom-howling Elsie and her whispering, sniveling husband—and hurried down the stairs in her bare feet. She trembled as she picked up the phone.

"I'm going to see Henry," said Liza's voice. "I thought you'd like to hear about it, afterward."

104

"I would, very much," said Ann.

"Did you sleep well?"

"Not very," Ann said.

"I lay awake for hours, thinking."

"I did, too."

"I knew you would, Ann."

Ann felt the husky voice come closer and Liza, herself, seemed to be at her side whispering into her ear. The voice was full of a coaxing quality, as if it were offering secrets to share rather than conversation.

"Sovey's letter," Ann thought. She couldn't hand it over to that groveling Sam Hartnett. Why not wait a day? Let Liza stay out of jail another day. And Henry *in* jail. It was only fair. She smiled at her new Olympian powers.

Liza continued, "I'll be home around four. If I'm not, the key to the front door is under the mat. Will you go in, Ann, and wait for me?"

"Yes."

"I looked for that lousy pistol for hours," Liza said. "Henry must have stuck it away somewhere."

"Of course. Do give him my love."

"I will."

"And tell him if he wants anything from the house, I'll be glad to bring it."

"I will, Ann." There was a giggle. "I almost wish we were going together. I'd like to hear him talk to both of us at once."

"That wouldn't be fair," said Ann, "to him."

"When was he ever fair to anybody?" Liza asked. There

was another small laugh. "I don't like to complain about your husband, Ann—but so help me God I haven't drawn a happy breath in five months. That's his idea of love— how miserable can he make a girl."

"Five months," thought Ann, "well, that's better than six."

"Did you get your lover boy home?" Liza asked.

"Oh, yes. He was quite docile."

"Take my advice, Ann, and throw him back to his wife. Strictly a mama's boy."

"Aren't they all?" she said.

"You're an ace," said Liza huskily. "Four o'clock?"

"I'll be there."

"Thanks." Liza breathed in silence for a moment. "Good-by." She hung up.

Ann remained motionless. Why did Liza want to see her? "Maybe she's pretending to be attracted," Ann thought. "They can put on an act, just as normal women do. She can't be really attracted. She must have some instincts about me. What I'm up to. Unless Lesbians are more naïve than other women. Or other men. Whichever it is." She thought about Lesbians. "I don't know anything about them, really. Except what I can guess. They must be a little like children." Liza seemed like a child. "Like children who are always eager to play. Because play is the only thing real to them. They have to pretend about everything else. Like Lesbians do about everything—but love." Ann's skin shivered. "*I'm* being stupid and naïve. She can't love me if she loves Henry. I'm thinking about the wrong things. If she

106

killed Sovey she's got only one thing on her mind—to stay free. And unsuspected. She knows Henry suspects her, or he wouldn't be lying to the police. And me, too. She may think I suspect. She may have looked in the laundry bag and found the letter gone. Then she'd know what I was up to. And want to see me. To get rid of me." Ann smiled. How could Liza kill her? Poison? Shooting? A sudden knife thrust? Ann laughed. It was silly. If Liza were guilty—and what else could she be?—the girl would take an entirely different tack. She'd try to get Henry's wife on her side, along with Henry. To help outwit the police. Or to help pay expenses for a trial. "That's why she's trying to charm me," Ann thought.

Her mind turned to Henry. How could Henry love a girl like that—coarse and promiscuous? He'd always disdained them, even before he was married. "There's no fun going to bed with a woman you can't corrupt." He couldn't possibly love Liza. "Except, of course, I don't know him. I only know what he's told me. My God, I know Liza better than I do Henry. She doesn't love *him*. The way she talked about him. She may even loathe him. But *he!* He's ready to go through all kinds of hell for her." Ann sighed. Another notion came to her, about why Henry was in jail. She considered it intently. Because it put him out of range of her tears, pain, hysteria. "I've found out about Liza and can't hit him over the head with a board." Henry's phrase. "I've got to do all my howling and recriminating out of earshot. On top of which I've even got to feel sorry for him. And worry about him. Because he's in jail, and in trouble. The unfaithful husband with the upper hand."

Walking upstairs, she was oddly without pain. As if things had cleared up. Henry was innocent and in trouble only because he was protecting Liza, and cleverly evading wifely retributions. What a complicated rottenness a man was. However, the police would straighten out the criminal thing. And get around to Liza, even without the Sovey letter. She thought, "I'll keep it, though, in case they don't." Poor Henry in jail was helping them both. She didn't want to wail over his betrayal of her, just yet. She entered the bedroom, not thinking to knock.

The tableau confused her. Elsie was sitting in the chair, her bodice unbuttoned. Sam was kneeling in front of her, hanging onto her with a drowning man's hand. His head was buried in her lap and he was sobbing loudly. Elsie, she noted, looked flush and smug, as if she had landed a muskellunge. She patted Sam's hand.

"I'm sorry," said Ann.

Elsie smiled vaguely. "Good God," Ann thought, "she hasn't seen or heard me. She's lost in a sexual trance."

Sam's wails of repentance increased. Elsie suddenly lifted Sam's tear-smeared face from her lap and pressed it against her breast. Ann stepped into the hall. She stood with her cheeks red, thinking, "She probably whips him, too. But forgot to bring her knout. That must be the secret of all those husbands Henry sneers at. They're masochists. Not just guilt complexes apologizing with mink coats and diamond bracelets. Elsie's loaded with them. But they get their kicks crawling at a woman's feet and getting the hell whaled out of them. And that dirty pervert Elsie! No wonder Henry has always sneered at her. And at all other Englewood wives like her. "The more moral front they put on, the more you can be sure they're hiding. These god damn Madam Virtues who wince at any hint of male and female buckety-buckety are all members of a sexual underground 'wanted' by the police."

Ann coughed, smiled, counted three and opened the door.

"Hello," she said. Elsie was buttoned up and standing. She looked very pretty—young, jolly and unwifely. Sam was not visible.

"Any good news?" Elsie asked.

"Not yet."

"I've decided to forgive Sam, in part," she said. "One must, you know. He's just a permissive weakling. Allowing himself to get drunk with the lowest kind of male companions. Professional sots. And letting some dirty little whore climb all over him with her dirty lips." Elsie smiled a Queen of Suburbia smile. "They're all spineless. I mean men. Poor Sam, he was going to give up the idea of running for mayor. I talked him out of it, I assure you."

"He'd make a fine mayor," said Ann.

"Englewood would be very lucky," said Elsie. She was "restoring" her face, like a pretty abbess at devotions. "Sam is certain he can get Henry out on bail after his hearing tomorrow. He's making a personal issue of it with the District Attorney."

Ann wondered where they'd got all this talk in.

"Yes," said Sam entering the room. "I'll have our Henry home in thirty-six hours."

Ann smiled and said, "That would be wonderful."

"Now tell me just what you want me to do, Ann," Elsie said. "I'm only here for your sake, darling."

Ann thought, "She's put her sex in a closet, like a vacuum cleaner that's done its job. That's what confuses a husband. There seem to be two women married to him—a shameless strumpet and a book of etiquette. Henry is right—wifehood is a dull sort of lunacy, a bourgeois schizophrenia."

She said aloud, "I'm seeing Henry around four. And I'd like to see him alone."

"I understand perfectly."

"If I could call you after five, Elsie."

"Perfect!" Elsie said. "I'll go to the hairdresser's now. And I'll be at our dressmaker's after five."

Sam beamed, "There goes another two hundred down the drain."

"Three hundred," said Elsie haughtily. She squeezed Ann's hand. Ann thought, "Madam's favors come high." A Henry remark came to her: "What a washout these black-mailing wives would be on the open market."

"Is there anything you have to talk to Ann about today?" Elsie looked imperiously at her husband.

"No, not a thing," Sam said, briskly. "Tell Henry he'll be out and home by tomorrow."

"I shall," said Ann.

"Too bad in a way," Elsie smiled. "It would do Henry so much good to stay in jail for a week longer. If it wasn't for

110

the social disgrace that *you* have to bear, darling." She patted Ann's arm.

"Let's hope Henry will have learned a little lesson when he comes out," Elsie said.

"He's a very bad student," Ann said, with an air of loyalty.

"They all are," said Elsie. "You know, darling, I've always been surprised that a woman as bright as you couldn't see through Henry." Ann frowned, "What an ass." Elsie continued, "Husbands can't stand being loved. It bores them. The more you love a man, the more he goes looking for somebody who has no use for him. Some silly whore who doesn't care if his head is on backward. I mean it, my dear. Men like to be mistreated."

"Because it gives them a chance to be honest," Ann said. "You can't be honest with someone who adores you."

"My point exactly," said Elsie. "Don't adore them. I'd lose Sam in a week if I started mooning over him."

"I doubt if you can keep a man faithful by not loving him," Ann said. "They have that exploring instinct. They like to poke around in new territory."

"Why, Ann!" her best friend cried, "I never knew you to be so utterly vulgar."

"Sorry," Ann said. "Having a husband in jail coarsens one."

"You sweet dear," Elsie embraced her shoulders. "You could never be coarse. Call me, my love, either at the hairdresser's, or join me at the dressmaker's."

She was still chatting as Ann said good-by in the hall.

A half-dozen jail officials were eager to help Liza King talk to inmate Henry Lawrence. They stood inhaling in her wake.

"Mr. Lawrence will be right along," said the short, bald cell guard. He stepped fifteen feet away and stood studying Mr. Lawrence's visitor as if he had heard about women but never seen one before.

Henry appeared behind the wire mesh. He was in shirt sleeves.

"Hello, darling," he said. "How are you?"

"I'm fine," said Liza. She beamed at him. "Can you see me smiling?"

"Yes," said Henry, "what in hell about?"

"Well, for one thing, your wife came to see me last night," said Liza. "We had supper at my place after the show."

"Good God," said Henry quietly.

"I suppose you're trembling."

"Go on," said Henry. "I'll tremble if there's any need to."

"One of you is a terrible liar," said Liza. Henry was silent. She continued, "I'm betting on you." Her voice became mocking. "You couldn't leave her because she adored you so. Because she was so good and pure. Jesus, men are liars. They'll lie about everything." Henry remained silent. "Well, why don't you ask me?" Liza demanded. She chuckled unexpectedly. "I won't rub it in too much, honey," she said. "I guess it's pretty hard for a husband to admit his wife is on the turf—like himself. Bouncing his name around in bed with other guys."

"Yes," said Henry, "it's not a nice thing to admit."

"You knew it," Liza said sharply. Henry was silent. "Of course you did," she continued. "Well, you'll have to think up another excuse for not leaving home now. I'm sure you won't have too much trouble finding one."

"So she confessed to you," Henry said.

"Confessed!" Liza chuckled. "She brought her boy friend along. Almost broke up my act with their ringside smooching."

"Sounds a little drunky," said Henry.

"Her friend was loaded," said Liza. "Ann was all right."

"Ann," Henry repeated the name as if surprised. "Which of her many admirers was on exhibit last night?"

"Sam somebody," said Liza. "He passed out on my bed. A real mess, snoring away with a face covered with lipstick."

"Sam," said Henry, and stopped.

"Know him?"

"Old pals," Henry smiled.

"Well, darling, I owe you a small apology."

"Good God, for what, my dear?"

"For not believing you weren't sleeping with her," Liza said. "But the odds were a thousand to one. She verified that side of your story."

"I'm glad," said Henry. He lit a cigarette. The wire mesh prevented Liza from noting the unprecedented tremble of his fingers.

"Except for the accidents," Liza added.

"What accidents?"

"Oh, stop it!" Liza's voice sharpened.

"I sincerely don't know what you mean," Henry said.

"You always denied it," said Liza. "Screamed and yelled you've never gone to bed with her since we fell in love. You swore on your life and my life."

"People are listening," said Henry.

"Let 'em," Liza said, "and you don't have to shake like a thief. The truth is a lot better than I ever figured it would be. I knew all the time two people can't live in the same house, and nothing goes on. Ann admitted it without my even asking."

"Admitted what?" Henry asked carefully.

"That you've slept with her a few times in the last six months. She called it 'accidents.'"

"Twice," said Henry firmly.

"Oh, what a bastard," Liza's voice was low, "accusing me of winking at Tony and you in the saddle all the time. What a rat," her voice was mild.

"I'm not in a position to argue," said Henry.

Liza smiled, and said suddenly, "You're cute."

"Thank you."

"Ann knows about your phone call to me. That night," Liza said. "She'd been out with her sweetie-man and heard you talking when she came in."

"Please," said Henry sharply, "I don't want to discuss it."

"Oh, he's jealous," Liza sneered.

"Naturally," Henry agreed.

"What a stinker you are!"

"Bulletin and new lead," said Henry with much irony.

"Hanky," Liza used her pet name for her tormentor. He answered softly, "Yes, doll?"

"I think I ought to tell Ann," she began, "about what happened."

"Don't be a damned idiot!" Henry said. "Tell her nothing."

"It'll be safer," Liza began.

"No! Not a word. To anybody!"

Liza was silent.

"Did this fellow Sam ask you any questions?"

"Why?" Liza whispered.

"Did he?"

"No," she said, "he was interested in mooey-mooey with Ann. He didn't even know I was around."

"Don't tell me that," Henry said. "He's the busiest billy goat of my rather large acquaintance. What did he ask you?"

"I told you. Nothing."

"Try to remember. It's important," he said softly. Liza was silent and then said, "You don't believe me."

"You haven't said anything yet."

"I don't mean about that jerk with your wife. I mean about me." Her voice was low. "You don't believe about Tom."

"Don't be stupid, my dear."

"You think I killed him," Liza said. "That's why you're

115

lying to the cops—about your not seeing him. To take the heat off me."

"True-blue Henry, the gun moll's pal."

"They know about your meeting Tom," said Liza. "It won't work, Henry."

Henry's voice was light, "Sweet Liza, I'll be happy to let you have my cell if the police insist."

"You think I did it," Liza said.

"No."

"Then why are you lying? Why do you want *me* to lie?"

"The natural instinct of an honest citizen," said Henry, "is to lie. Particularly when his honesty is in question."

"Talk straight," said Liza.

"All right. Show me how—by answering my question."

"What question?"

"About Sam," Henry said. "Did he make a pass at you?"

Liza's voice rose. "For God's sake! Are you going to start in on that jerk?"

"My dear, if he's good enough for my wife, he can't be entirely unworthy of your notice."

"You're trying to get me sore," Liza glared. "I don't know why. Except you like to hurt me."

"I keep hoping you'll say something truthful in your pain."

Liza smiled. "You're kidding. Because you're upset about being in jail. I'm sorry."

"Thank you."

"Really, about that fellow Sam, I don't see how a girl

like Ann can go into the hay with such a drip. You must have driven her to it."

"Ann was never choosy," he answered. "First come, first served was always her love slogan."

"I don't believe it," Liza said. "He's got a belly, too."

"Maybe she likes that," said Henry. "Women develop queer fetishes as they mature."

"You're pretty vicious," she said. "And I know why. Because you're hurt. You didn't know about Fatso Sam. You thought you had both of us sitting up faithfully on our hind legs. Furthermore, I don't believe her either."

"About what, my dear?"

"Those two accidents. Twenty I'll bet you. Or maybe two hundred. You're both lying to me."

"Darling, I must defend my wife. She's a terribly truthful woman."

"Maybe," said Liza and smiled. "I hope so. Henry—please let's both be sensible about that night. And let me handle it my way—with Frankie?"

"Who in hell is Frankie?"

"Sergeant Frank Davies. The one who arrested you. For murder. Remember?" She smiled.

"Good God," Henry glared through the wire mesh. "I didn't notice his name. That's your cop sweetie."

"Was," said Liza.

"Let's not argue about tenses," he scowled. "You're not very good at them."

"You rat," said Liza.

"Officer Davies, your sobbing lover," Henry said. "Heart-broken Frankie. And I didn't catch on."

"You'll make up for lost time," said Liza, bitterly.

"And now you're dying to talk to your sweet copper, aren't you?"

"I loathe him," said Liza.

"Loathing usually throws you right into a man's arms," said Henry.

"You're worse than he is," she whispered, "sadists, both of you! Dirty sadists!"

"Nice for you to have two of them on tap, my dear."

"Look, you stupid sonofabitch," Liza said quietly, "I'll walk out of this jail and you'll never see me again, if you don't cut it out about Frank."

"Go on, go back to him," said Henry, quietly.

There was silence. Liza stood motionless. Henry blew smoke through the wire wall. She said, finally, "I want to get you out of this."

"Don't worry about me."

"And get myself out," said Liza.

"You *are* out," he whispered. "Just stay there."

"Did you hide my gun anyplace?"

"Yes," said Henry. "In the bottom bureau drawer."

"Thank God," she smiled. "Henry, I'm seeing Ann this afternoon. What should I tell her?"

"Nothing, baby."

Liza smiled. "Do you want me to pump her for the names of all her lovers?"

Henry was silent.

"I still can't believe it about her," Liza said.

Henry said, "You mustn't be fooled by the fancy store front. The same goods are on sale inside." He laughed. "Darling, I adore you."

"Do you? Honestly?"

"Madly."

"It's hard to believe," she sighed.

"What about you?" he asked softly.

"I don't know," Liza said. "I guess I've cooled off for a while."

"What a bitch," he whispered.

"I'm sure it'll come back, Hank."

"It was never there."

"Oh, don't start that!" she frowned. "All I mean about being cooled off is that you haven't been torturing me for three days. And I feel a little human, for a change. Please don't mind."

"I don't mind anything," Henry answered. "If you get lonely for a little torture I'm sure Sergeant Davies will be able to oblige."

"What a filthy bastard you are," said Liza. Her voice rose. "No man has touched me. Since you. Or can. Or can even get near me. And you know it!"

"Why come here and tell me you've cooled off?" asked Henry. "That's all I need to make my cell comfy."

"Darling," said Liza, "just talking to you drives me crazy with feeling." Her voice was husky. "Can't you tell?"

"Yes."

"Henry, please let me see your lawyer."

"No, listen," Henry was stern, "listen to me. Not a word to anyone. You swear?"

"I swear," said Liza.

"Time's up," said the guard. "But you can have another five minutes."

He squirmed wistfully.

"Thank you," said Henry through the mesh, "but we're through."

"O.K.," said the guard, "this way."

"Good-by," Liza said to the vague face behind the wire mesh. "Any message for Ann?"

There was a pause.

"Keep away from her," Henry said.

"Why?"

"She's a bad influence on you," Henry said, "liable to put wrong ideas into your innocent head."

"You sarcastic bastard," Liza's voice was gentle.

"Good-by, darling," said Henry. "And no talking."

"Mum," said Liza. She smiled intently at the dim face and turned away.

On her way out, Liza looked into the warden's office to thank him for his courtesy.

"Happy to be of service. Any time," the gloomy-looking official said. Sergeant Davies stepped toward her.

"I want to talk to you, Liza," he said.

He walked out into the lobby, taking her arm.

"Let go of me," Liza said.

"We'll go somewhere," said the blond sergeant. "I want to talk to you."

"We'll go nowhere," she said.

"For your own good," his voice was low and pleading.

"Oh, stop it," she said.

"I mean it," the sergeant said. "It's important. We'll go to my place." He looked at her silent, rigid face. "I'm giving you a last chance. Don't turn it down, Liza. Don't. Don't turn it down."

"If you don't take your hand off me, I'll start yelling."

"Take it easy, honey," Davies said in his low voice.

"I told you to keep away from me," Liza said.

"So I have, honey."

"Forever," said Liza.

"You don't mean that, honey."

"I mean it, Frank."

"No, no," his voice was eager. "Take it back. I'll give you a chance to take it back."

"I take nothing back," she looked contemptuously into his eyes. "You're disgusting. You've always disgusted me. Now let go my arm. Or I yell."

Sergeant Davies let the arm go.

"Thank you," Liza said.

The sergeant's face was pink. His eyes were almost closed. They were alone in the building entrance.

"I'm sorry you want it like that, honey," Davies said.

"You nutty junkie," she glared, "you're full of hop or you wouldn't talk to me."

Sergeant Davies smiled. His eyes opened. "I can nail you," he said quietly. "For keeps. Maybe that's the best thing for you and me. I nail you."

121

"Nice to have seen you again, Sergeant," Liza smiled.

"You godam Lesbian stallion," Sergeant Davies said softly, "the pleasure's been all mine." He grinned at her. "Or maybe it's going to be pretty soon."

Liza walked out of the jail without further words. It was always the same with Frank—an angry clown of a man. You could feel sorry for him if he'd let you. God knows he whimpered enough. But he wouldn't let you. "Always wanting to scare you into something," she thought. "The hell with him."

She took a taxi and sat smiling at a suddenly infatuated driver, who was willing to bet she was in show business. Walking up the stairs to her apartment, Liza remembered the blond sergeant again and frowned. "If worst comes to worst, I'll look him up," she thought, "the poor sap." She remembered his weeping and banging his head against the wall. "Hardly a year ago," she thought. "He can't have changed too much."

The key was missing from under the door mat. Liza pressed the bell. Ann opened the door.

"Hello," said Ann. "I got here early from the hair-dresser's."

"I'm glad," said Liza. She threw her purse in a chair. "Had lunch?"

"Yes."

"What a lovely outfit," Liza smiled. "You look like a kid."

Ann was wearing a clinging summer print silk dress. It made her look boneless.

"I'll get out of this harness," said Liza and started to

remove her gray suit. She went behind a screen at the other end of the studio room.

"She's modest," Ann thought, and waited. Liza came out in a soft, plain robe of white.

"That's kind of mysterious," Liza said. "Henry told me he put the gun in the bureau drawer. It isn't there. Have a drink with me?"

"Yes."

"Anything special?"

"Whatever you take," said Ann.

"Gin," Liza smiled, "the chorus girl's friend. I don't know how to make a Martini. Just sugar and lemon."

"That's fine," said Ann.

Liza talked as they drank.

"Henry was a little jumpy," she said. "So was I. It wasn't a very pleasant visit," she smiled at her guest. "You know, I'm not madly in love with your husband today. I told him that."

"It must have upset him," said Ann.

"Everything upsets Henry," Liza said. "He's just as critical about mad love as about no love. My God, what a critic that boy is!"

Ann thought, "If she's found out Sovey's letter's gone, she must suspect me." Another thought surprised her—"Of what? I'm not doing anything about it. Good lord, she may think it's because I—I'm attracted, or something."

"I met Frank Davies in the jail," Liza said, "as I was leaving." Ann looked blank. "He's the sergeant on the case. I used to know him. That's the cop I told you about."

"Oh, the man you once loved," said Ann, "who hurt you so."

"He didn't hurt me," said Liza.

Ann watched her sit down a few feet away and thought, "No laying on of hands like last night. She's too upset. It must be hard to feel sensual with a murder on your conscience. If she has a conscience."

"I'd love to talk to you," Liza said. "I've never had a girl friend to talk to. Except one. And—well, that was a different kind of talk."

"About Henry?" Ann asked.

"No, no," said Liza. "About me. I'm upset. Horribly. Last night after you left, I kept wanting to go up to some high roof and jump off. Jump like hell."

"Because you're worried over Henry," Ann sighed. "I understand."

"No, not Henry," said Liza. "Or maybe yes. In an involved way. I've been like this before. Long before Henry. I tried to cut my wrists when I was sixteen."

"Good God, why?" Ann stared.

"Because I hated men," said Liza. "And they started coming at me. It was like finding yourself in a barrel of mice. I ran away from home with one of them when I was sixteen."

"Dear me," Ann thought, "it's like Henry telling me about the fat woman in the circus who raped him when he was a boy. I wonder if he told her."

"The home I ran away from," said Liza, "was an orphan home. They used to farm me out as a dishwasher and sweeper-upper until they began to get too many complaints.

The complaints began when I was thirteen. I was fully developed, so to speak—at that age."

"I don't understand," said Ann, and looked very suburban.

"The ladies of the house," said Liza, "would catch their husbands groping me. And file a complaint."

"Oh. I see."

"So I skipped off with a young man. No love. Nothing. Except that it was better than washing dishes. And being groped by retired letter carriers. I'll skip down a few years in my confessions. Do you mind talking like this?"

"No," said Ann, "it's terribly interesting." She remembered the early wedlock months and Henry's slow and detailed revelations of her predecessors. Strumpets and stylish ladies who had wallowed in all manner of beds with him. They had fascinated her for two years, at least, like a troupe of ghostly Scheherazades come to entertain her with presexual overtures.

"Frank Davies was really the first one that mattered," said Liza. "He was a dedicated policeman. Spent all his time reading. Or working out in a gym to improve his muscles. Mad about improvements, Frankie. He was planning a big career. Sergeant, lieutenant, captain and chief Mucky-Muck. He had the schedule all down."

Liza sighed. "Damn, I hate to remember him," she said.

"Don't," said Ann.

"I want to," Liza smiled brightly. "It relaxes me. That's one of my troubles—I never remember anything. Everything that happens falls down a well. Frankie was an orphan, like me. Only much worse. He remembered his mother. And, oh what a bitch she was. A crazy hoppie. Worked in some movie publicity department, off and on. When she had a job she'd pull Frankie out of his orphanage and share a room with him. Except when she had customers."

"Customers?" Ann queried.

"She was a whore, sort of," said Liza. "She used to put Frankie outside on the steps. In the snow usually. Until her gentleman caller left. Then she'd bring him in."

"How old was he?"

"He was around ten when his ma finally disappeared," said Liza. "You'd think it would be good riddance. But he must have been a screwy kid. He hollered for a whole year. They had to keep him in the orphanage hospital."

Liza poured more drinks.

"He wanted to marry me," she said. "Please forget those lies I told you about him. Poor Frank. He was scared to death of sex. He didn't hate it as I did. Although I learned to sort of ignore it while it was going on. Frank was hungry for it—but frightened."

"Of what?"

"Impotence," said Liza. "He was always terrified in advance that he'd be no good. He'd made a number of tries before me. All strike-outs. Some dames even laughed at him. One of them drove him crazy. She said, "Listen, Mister, don't come back again.""

"But he's so virile looking," said Ann. "In fact, I found him a little repulsive for that reason. Because he seemed like some thick, insensitive rapist."

"Bushwa," said Liza. "He'd rather grab a hot stove than

a dame. I did all the raping with him. And it worked. He went crazy over me. I'd made him into a man. And—you can imagine. He kept after me day and night, laughing, tumbling me over on chairs, on the floor—anyplace we could be reasonably alone for a half hour."

"Why wouldn't you marry him?" Ann asked.

"Because there was a cold spot in me toward Frank," said Liza. "Oh, it wasn't in the usual place. But here." She touched her bosom. "Maybe it was because he was a cop. And something in me didn't like cops. No. That wasn't it. I might as well tell you the truth. Another drink?"

"Yes," said Ann. She was shivering inside. "She frightens me," Ann thought, "in a funny way. Because she's playing cat and mouse with me. Maybe she thinks I'm a Lesbian and that I'll grab her and start moaning over her. She's crazy."

Ann smiled and sipped her second drink. Liza continued, "My glands worked nicely and Frank was very pleased with himself. But sex isn't only a few glands functioning. It has to be in your guts and brain and all over you to count. With Frank I was just localized. Then I met the Princess. And found out about myself."

"Oh," said Ann. Her throat and mouth felt dry, despite the gin.

"I was singing at The Flamingo," said Liza, "a plushy joint. The Princess used to appear every night. At a table in the back. With a sort of distinguished-looking old boy for an escort. One of those old diplomat types who look like boiled celery up close. Oh, I'd love to tell you, Ann. It'll

127

help me." She reached over and gripped Ann's hand. Ann squeezed the warm fingers. "Do tell me," she said. "I'm fascinated."

"I joined them for a drink after the show one night," said Liza. "We sat in the dim light at the back. The Princess was Russian. Dark haired and sort of heavy featured but with large, fine eyes and remarkable eyebrows like large charcoal smears. Well, it became a habit—my joining them after my number. And Tanya used to sit silent and smiling at me and holding a rose as if she were posing for some old-fashioned portrait. She would drop off one of her slippers and caress my ankle with her soft foot. And Oscar, that was her friend, would keep on talking, telling stories about the old days in Romania. I fell in love with Tanya. So madly in love that I thought I'd die if she didn't love me back. If she didn't want me. Another drink, Ann?"

Ann held out her glass. "She's trying to excite me like Henry used to," she thought, "with play by play sex details of other loves. She can't be as truthful as she sounds. There's something behind her talk. As if she were trying to suck me into something. Why should she want to commit suicide last night, after hearing that Henry was all hers? Because of the murder, of course. The murder."

"She wanted me," said Liza. "I was in heaven. She wasn't beautiful. But I would almost faint when she touched me. I'd sit waiting for her to ask me to touch her. Oh, yes, I forgot to say—I ran away from Frank. Tanya had a nice place in Long Island. I went to live with her and Oscar. Although he didn't figure. Just sort of an onlooker."

Liza smiled. Her face had a peaceful look, like that of a child lost in memories. Ann shivered. The dryness went from her throat. Her lips felt moist and her eyes became clouded as if with tears. "She's mad," she thought. "She's trying to turn me into the Princess. If there was a Princess."

Liza talked on, "My affair with Tanya lasted a whole summer. It was the only happy time I'd ever known. It was wonderful, every day. Every night. She barely let me alone. And I didn't want to be let alone. I lost weight. I became so exhausted I could hardly walk. I lost interest in eating. I wanted only love. Or whatever it was. It was the same every time. Always knocked me out. Shook me. Made me scream and fall apart weeping. I was so wonderfully tormented. I kept crying like a crazy baby.

"I'd forgotten there'd ever been a Frank Davies. But he finally ran me down. He was always a smart cop. And he still is, the sonofabitch. He came just at the right time, too. Tanya and Oscar were going back to her estate in Romania. They had fixed things up with some Commie big shots. And Tanya had told me I couldn't come with her. Just like that. No explanations. No alibiing. Just—no more me.

"Well, Frank found me bawling like a loony. And started accusing me. In a way he saved my life. I got so godam mad at him that the pain of Tanya ditching me got mixed up. Frank took me to his flat where I lay sick for a week. And he started begging. Not for me only. For his manhood back. I should give it back to him. I gave him nothing. I laughed."

"But why?" Ann asked.

129

"I don't know," said Liza. "Because I'm a bitch. Mean. Vicious. And sore. I took it all out on him, I guess."

"Sore about what?" Ann asked softly.

"About being alive, I guess," Liza smiled. "Don't ask me more. I don't know the details. I read a poem once—Henry read me a poem once about death—somebody dying and wrapping themselves up in dreams and lying down very stylish on a couch. I loved it. I love death."

She looked boldly into Ann's eyes. "Do you?"

"No," said Ann. "What a thing to love!"

Liza sighed. "Well, I finally was able to navigate and left Frank's place and moved in here. But there was no shaking him. He followed me. So I laughed some more. I told him all about Tanya. How I'd worshiped her. And Frank sat crying and banging his head against the wall. That wall, right there."

She pointed.

"Good lord," Ann stared, as if something were happening in the room.

"Then he went for the dope," Liza said. "He had a lot of connections, being highly regarded as a cop. And he started socking himself with the junk. Mostly heroin or cocaine.

"One night he came in here very high. He was going to kill us both with his cop's gun, him and me. I told him to go ahead. I told him I'd heard that impotent men got a big kick out of shooting off a gun that could work. Yes, I stood right here. And laughed. Jesus, I wanted him to do it. Kill me. Put me away. But all I got was a beating. He punched the hell out of me and then ran out."

Liza smiled suddenly, and added as if it were the topper of a joke, "And Tom Sovey ran in."

She laughed. "It wasn't much of a change," she said. "From one hop head to another. And the same basic deficiency as a lover. I think I actually met Tom through Frank. Tom was physically a pip-squeak alongside Frank. A poor foolish ham actor with the monkey on his back. It's funny. Frank wasn't jealous of him. He even used to like him. I guess it had something to do with Tom's dope ring connections. And because Tom was less interested in sex than in walking on his hands."

Ann thought, "She's frightened. She doesn't want to be alone. She's afraid they'll come and arrest her."

The telephone rang.

"Hello," said Liza. "Yes, it is. . . . Who is this? . . . Oh, just a moment."

She covered the phone and turned to Ann, "It's Mr. Hartnett. Are you here?"

"Yes," said Ann. "Hello, Sam," she said into the phone.

"Ann," Sam said quickly. "I can't talk over the phone. But get away as fast as you can. It's very important. And come home. Leave in five minutes. It's important."

"Thank you, Sam," Ann smiled. "I'll be there."

She hung up and looked at Liza's strong teeth in her wide, smiling mouth.

"Please forgive me," Ann said. "I must go. I hope you understand."

"I don't," said Liza.

"He's waiting for me."

"I don't believe it," said Liza. Her neck was arched, her bosom lifted.

"Believe what?" Ann asked.

"You and that fellow Sam," Liza answered. "But you don't have to tell me any truths. Thanks for listening to my long, sad story."

"Thanks for telling it to me," said Ann.

Liza moved toward her. Her eyes shone, her lips were moist and parted.

"Ann," she said huskily. The beggar sound was in her voice. Her body seemed to soften as she stood before Ann, arms hanging limply—"as if she were naked," Ann thought.

"I must go, Liza," she said.

Liza was silent and waiting.

"I'll call you tomorrow," Ann said and stopped. Liza's eyes were full of tears. They blurred the large blue pupils. They ran into the wide mouth and glistened on the thick lips.

"Oh, my God," Ann thought, "I can't let her go on like this. I must do something."

She stared at the tear-wetted face and its pleading silence.

"I hope you feel better tomorrow, Liza," she said. A gaiety was suddenly in her spirit.

"You've ruined your make-up," Ann said. Her voice was cool and amused. "Good-by."

She was out of the door. She walked down the stairs without looking back at the queerly limp figure watching her with falling tears.

Englewood on a summer afternoon was a reassuring stretch of Americana. Its fine lawns and semimodest mansions testified that all was well in the world of advertising executives, corporation counsels and stock exchange gamblers.

Driving through its precise and tree-shaded streets, Ann wondered why Henry had chosen this bland little area of respectability as a home base. Only the latest automobile models were visible in its highways. Its expensive-looking houses and people seemed also the latest thing in existence —turned out in stylish and uniform lots.

When they had bought their house six years ago, Henry had said, "We will be happy here in our old age. There will be no hint of youth around us to remind us we lost something."

She thought of Liza. "I'm glad I didn't turn in the Sovey letter. She's a weirdie. How can a man stand all that craziness. And frigidity. She's obviously frigid." She recalled a sentence out of Balzac about a supposed Don Juan: "There was so much fire in his eyes, it was unlikely that it would be duplicated elsewhere."

Sam's car was parked in the Lawrence driveway.

"If that idiot starts wrestling again, I'll kick him in the groin," Ann frowned. She entered her home a little fiercely.

Sam, alone, stood waiting the living room.

"I'm very glad you came," he said smugly. "Thank you, my dear Ann."

133

"Where's Elsie?"

"Shopping," Sam answered.

"Look—before you tell me anything," Ann said, "last night never happened. And never will again."

Sam nodded, "I feel just as you do."

"What an insufferable oaf," Ann thought. "No wonder Elsie beats him. That's all he's good for. A human rug."

"I want you to know," Sam said, "that my respect for you is a thousand per cent. And that you're a fine woman in my eyes."

"Oh, shut up," Ann said. "Let's talk about something decent. What's happened? Why did you track me down?"

"Henry's free," said Sam. "I called you at Miss King's because I didn't want Henry to walk in on both of you. I thought it would just create unnecessary embarrassment."

Ann thought, "Henry headed straight for Liza."

"Also," Sam said, "that woman's dangerous."

"In what way?"

"I didn't think you ought to be alone with her."

"You have a rotten filthy mind, Sam!" Ann said, "a real Englewood brain."

He stared at her.

"If you're referring to last night," he said, "I've apologized. And I'll apologize again. Please don't hold it too much against me. Remember, I was fairly well stewed."

"Oh, nuts!" Ann cried. "You really make me sick with your all-around all-American cringing."

"I don't consider doing the right thing is cringing," said

134

Sam. Ann wanted to answer with obscene words but stayed silent. "I take the full blame for the other night."

"Well, you're a godam fool if you do," Ann said.

"No, Ann, it's always the man's fault," Sam was firm. "Men have that side to them. It gets out of hand some-times." He held out his hand. "Forgiven?"

"Forgiven," Ann said.

"All I meant about Liza King is that she's liable to be a dangerous person when cornered. And I'd rather you weren't on the premises when the police cornered her."

"Care for a drink?" Ann asked.

"No thank you, Ann." He looked out of the window. "Henry ought to be along soon. And, by the way, before he comes I'd like to solicit your support."

"I told you I won't tell Elsie," Ann said irritably.

"Not that, not that," Sam said. "I've decided to run for mayor of Englewood. Elsie thinks it would be the right thing to do, and fun for all of us."

"You'd make a superb mayor," said Ann. "Who knows? You might even end in the White House."

"I know you're joking but thanks just the same," said Sam. "I'll put you on the Woman's Committee."

"That'll be nice," said Ann. "Now tell me about Liza King. Do the police feel sure she killed Sovey?"

"Yes, positive," said Sam. "I had an hour's talk with the D.A. He admitted the case against Henry didn't hold water. But most of the credit for Henry's getting out belongs to Sergeant Davies. The one who questioned you yesterday. A remarkable man and a first-rate detective. I don't think he's closed his eyes for forty-eight hours. He kept after the evidence like a bloodhound."

"What evidence?" Ann asked, and thought of Henry. "I wonder how long Liza will detain him. Or he her." She felt no pain with the query. "It doesn't matter any more," she thought. "He's more a fool than a villain." This finding surprised her. Henry had never been a fool once in their eight years together.

"I met Davies in the jail," Sam was explaining. "We both talked to Henry. And, thank God, he stopped his lying. Davies presented him with facts, of course, that he couldn't lie away."

"I'm glad I didn't have to turn in that Sovey letter," Ann thought.

"Davies' evidence was conclusive of Henry's innocence," Sam said. "After Henry left the San Mareno Hotel he ran into Sovey in the street. They went to a nearby bar and Henry gave Sovey a hundred dollars."

"Blackmail," said Ann.

"Exactly," said Sam. "A bartender and two customers saw the transaction. The sergeant has their statements. Henry left Sovey and came straight home. But Sovey went off looking for some dope. He was a drug addict. He'd been trying to buy some heroin on credit for two weeks. Well, he got a hundred dollars' worth that night. And all hopped up, he called on Liza. Davies has the cab driver's statement who drove Sovey to Liza's building. He has also statements from two of Liza's neighbors across the hall. They heard Liza King screaming at Sovey and threatening to

136

break his head if he didn't go away. And stay away. One of
the neighbors—a young girl—heard Sovey yelling at Miss
King that she was a no-good bitch and a dirty home-
wrecker. And he wasn't going to let her get away with it
—this time."

"An unexpected ally," said Ann.

"Tom Sovey was Liza King's husband," said Sam. "He'd
been blackmailing her for several months."

"How disgusting," Ann murmured.

"Yes," said Sam, "hard to visualize a woman like that
being anybody's wife."

"Much too proud for that kind of bondage," Ann said.
She blushed at this spontaneous statement, and thought, "I
can't possibly feel friendly toward a murderess. And Henry's
anaconda." But she did.

"Now, wait a minute," Sam smiled, "we both know some
pretty proud women who happen to be wives."

"Name one," said Ann.

"Two," Sam said, proudly. "You and Elsie."

"Elsie is a pious payroll bandit," said Ann, "and I'm worse.
A wife who lets her best friend's husband paw her black
and blue for five hours."

"Ann," Sam's voice was firm, "you mustn't punish yourself like that. We did nothing."

"I enjoy your genius for hypocrisy," said Ann. "You ought
to go far as a politico. In either party."

"It's not hypocrisy, Ann," Sam said, "it's siding with one's
better self."

"Yes, Henry's good at that, too," Ann smiled, and quoted

him: "It's not what you do that counts, but what you are."
She added on her own, "The husband's alibi for his wandering libido."

"Ann," Sam frowned, "you're too nice to talk like that."

"I'm the un-nicest, no good, wallowing bitch in Englewood," said Ann, "which is a large boast. What a pack of French whores in Mother Hubbards." She was thinking of Elsie. "But let's be good Americans, and forget it." She smiled blandly. "Tell me about who killed Tom Sovey."

Sam answered the question, gratefully. "When Henry called Miss King from Englewood, the night of the murder, Sovey was still with her. He was doped to the ears. He grabbed the phone from her and started laying down the law as her husband. What you heard and couldn't remember was Henry talking to Sovey as well as Liza. Calling him by name. So you knew Henry was innocent because he was talking to a Sovey still alive when Henry came home to sleep."

"My logical subconscious," Ann said. "But what evidence is there against Miss King?"

"Just the murder gun," said Sam. "The police found it buried in a flowerpot in the apartment."

"That's mad!"

"A gun is a pretty difficult piece of evidence to remove," said Sam. "There's always somebody bound to be looking when you drop it off a ferryboat or leave it in a public toilet."

"Her gun. Really?"

"Yes," Sam said. "With one bullet missing. Same caliber that killed Sovey. And a test showed the gun was fired recently. Less than four days ago. The gun clinches the case against Liza King."

"She kept the gun under her bed," Ann said. "Henry put it in a bureau drawer. And she couldn't find it. She was looking for it yesterday."

"She didn't have to look. She knew where it was," said Sam. "She was just setting you up as a prospective witness."

Ann frowned. "Then the police think Miss King chased Mr. Sovey all the way back to his hotel, shot him, and then ran home and buried the murder weapon in a flowerpot on her premises. It seems a little odd."

"Murder is usually a little odd," said Sam. "Liza King shot Sovey in her apartment. The wounds weren't immediately fatal. And he was full of cocaine. She put the gun in the flowerpot meaning to dispose of it later. The hopped-up Sovey went away and headed for his hotel. He collapsed in the alley and died."

"But he would have bled all over the place," Ann said.

"The coroner's physician says the bleeding was internal," said Sam. "Davies has the report. And about that muffler with the bloodstains—"

"You told them!"

"The only thing to do," Sam smiled. "Before Henry left Miss King's place, they had a fearful row. She threw a chair at him."

"A row over what?" Ann asked.

"It's not important."

"It is," said Ann.

"Well, let's be adult about it, then," said Sam. "A row

139

over the usual thing. His having to leave her and go home to his wife. She grabbed Henry and while she struggled, she developed a bad nosebleed and it got on Henry's muffler."

"While he was comforting her," said Ann.

"Henry admitted everything," said Sam, "when he finally started talking. He had been covering up for Miss King. About Sovey being at her place when he called from here."

"Have they arrested Miss King yet?" Ann asked.

"Sergeant Davies is after her," Sam smiled. "And, by George, I'd hate to have him after me."

Henry walked into the room.

"There's no place like home," he looked at the two mockingly. "If I'm not in the way."

"I didn't expect you so soon," said Ann.

"Miss King wasn't in," Henry said. "I hung around for fifteen minutes and left."

"She'll be sorry to have missed you," Ann said.

Henry looked out of a window. "He's thinner," Ann thought, "and different." She wondered at her aloofness.

"Sit down, Sam," said Henry. "I want to confer with you. Both of you."

Henry rummaged a desk for pipe and tobacco.

"First, I want to talk about Liza King," Henry went on. "They're going to arrest her for Sovey's killing. I'm certain she didn't do it. And I'm not running out on her. I intend to finance her defense, if she's tried. And I intend to testify in her behalf."

140

"Do you mind if I go upstairs," said Ann, "and leave you two Galahads to thresh things out?"

"You're not going upstairs," said Henry. He looked at her pleadingly, despite the anger in his voice. "There's something different," Ann thought. The slightly rumpled hair, lean El Greco face, derisive eyes and fine waistline were still there. But the man who combined them seemed absent. "As if he'd got religion," Ann thought. She frowned at this. A pious Henry would be the last straw.

"I've been sitting in a lousy jail cell for two days pondering my sins," said Henry, "and other people's sins as well. Before I get around to my *mea culpa* I'd like to clear up the case of My Wife and My Best Friend and their Kissing Bug spree."

"He hasn't changed too much," thought Ann.

"Look, Henry, I'm exhausted," said Sam. "I've been slugging away all day in your behalf."

"Thank you," Henry said, "I have no complaints to find with you as a lawyer. But as my best friend you seem a bit miscast, Mr. Hartnett."

"I can't believe my ears," said Ann. "A Henry come to judgment. Good God!"

"Good God, yourself!" said Henry, "smooching with Sam in public like a pair of juvenile delinquents! What if someone from Englewood had seen you?"

"Oh, for heaven's sake!" Ann frowned. "Don't pretend you don't know. Miss Liza King told you. It was an act. For your sake and nobody else's."

"A lot of lipstick changed places, I hear," said Henry. "Somebody was overacting."

A reddened Sam turned his back and looked out of a window.

"What a cad you are," said Ann, "coming home with accusations. You who've been slithering around with your anaconda for five months. Bouncing into her bed every day. And moaning lies to her that you were through with me sexually. Assuring her I was the untouched wife. Me! With my back aching from your lechery. What a monster!"

"Nevertheless," Henry repeated firmly, "there was considerable overacting. I'm a villain and a thorough bastard. We'll go into my case in a moment. But before I'm hanged by my thumbs, I'd like a statement on the other matter. Of my wife and best friend."

"Love to make it," Ann smiled. "I got Sam drunk and led him on to kiss and paw me and dragged him to the café so Liza could see him loving me up and think I was a wanton bitch like herself. And then get her to talk to me. And confide in me."

"Very good," said Henry. "Did your plot include a bed? Or did you indoctrinate Mr. Hartnett on the sofa?"

"I ought to slap your stupid face," said Ann, and laughed. "I'm sorry," she added. "I'm not laughing at you, Henry. I'm laughing at Sam."

"He wasn't acting," said Henry.

"No," said Ann, "he was very sincere. And madly in love with me. Until this morning. When he started crawling at Elsie's feet. And weeping on her bosom—while she was kicking him. They had a lovely time—and in my favorite chair."

"It's a lie!" Sam cried. "The whole godam thing's a lie. I told Elsie the truth!"

"Go home, you fool!" Ann said. "I'm not going to tell Elsie on you. Just Henry. I like you boys to know each other. But I'll not snitch to the Wives' Union."

"I'll see you tomorrow, Sam," Henry said. "I want you to handle Liza's case."

"You don't have to pay him anything," said Ann. "I can just blackmail him."

"I was drunk last night," Sam said, "and if you want to believe what Ann says, go ahead. Personally, I don't remember a godam thing. As I told Elsie."

"That's the best way," said Henry. "What we don't remember can't hurt us. *Adios,* see you tomorrow."

Sam walked briskly out of the room.

"What a yellow dog," Henry puffed his pipe. "Husbands are all yellow dogs. Me included."

Ann was silent.

"I've had quite a look at myself the last few days," he continued morosely, "a sort of Hogarth series." She was silent. "The 'Rake's Progress,'" he added.

"I know the series," Ann said.

"Growing a conscience at my age is a bit uncomfortable," Henry said. "I've used yours for so long. Much easier to outwit."

Ann thought, "He's going to woo me with confessions. And try to get me into bed before dinner." She recalled angrily that he had been able to quiet her half-formed suspicions during the past five months by well-timed sexual assaults. Her wifely queries always turned into sighs of pleasure.

"I hope you don't start crying," said Henry, "because I want to say a lot of things, clearly. For both our sakes."

"I don't feel like crying," Ann looked at him intently. "I don't feel like anything. I don't feel like myself."

"Shock," said Henry.

"Maybe."

"We'll skip the nonsense about you and Sam," he went on. "I just wanted to annoy that drooling boy scout." He smiled. "I believe you. And I believe in you."

"Do you? How nice," she looked boldly at him. "It was rather fun—for a while." He was silent. "You were almost right about the sofa. I was heading for it like a homing pigeon. Sam spoiled it all by—a change of rhythm."

"Are you trying to excite me?" Henry asked.

"Does my getting sexual with another man have that effect on you?"

"Don't be a hypocrite," said Henry. "I've driven you crazy talking about other women. And their salutes to Eros. I remember your interest in my nymphomaniac cousin Hildegard. The one who insisted on—"

"Shut up!" Ann interrupted.

"Sorry," said Henry, "but a chaste wife who has tasted unchastity is terribly appealing." Ann wondered why. "The books say it's a sort of carom-shot homosexuality," Henry continued, "but I doubt if that's true—with me." He smiled tenderly. "I was just hoping that any sin you may have

144

committed or almost committed would sort of lessen your horror of me—and my sins. I'd like a friend in court—even Sam Hartnett. I love you."

Ann was silent.

"Thank you for not making all the obvious answers," Henry went on. "Darling, it's hard to explain about Liza."

"I don't want any explanations."

"Perhaps I can make them interesting," said Henry, "and even amusing."

"Amusing!" she stared at him.

"The truth about a man's sexual didoes is usually on the funny side," said Henry, "if I can tell the truth. I'll try. I promise I won't make up any fairy tales to soothe you." He paused, pondered, and said slowly, "Liza roused a side of me I didn't think existed any more. The sex-psychologist. She sort of turned me into a bedroom professor. With a class in messed up libido. It used to be my favorite subject. Any girl with sexual complications and a broken-glass psyche always stirred my instincts for research."

Ann bit her lip to stop a smile.

"I told you truth was always a bit clownish," said Henry, "but honestly, that's the way I used to be. Neurotic, dishonest, phony ladies always fascinated me. Not crawling into their beds, particularly. That was a side line. But crawling into their minds. Going after their lies and secrets like a prosecuting attorney. That was Liza's appeal. I say 'was' because she hasn't got it any more. There's no mystery left in her. I know her. Case closed."

Ann was silent and without thought. She sat aloof in a

strange house listening to a stranger. An amusing stranger.

"The point I want to make," said Henry, "is that I've changed. Not only about Liza. But about myself. Please believe me."

"I'm sorry," said Ann, "but I can't believe anything you say. I don't know what else has happened, but my credulity has been shocked out of me."

"I'd like to put it back," said Henry.

"You're not a clever enough liar—any more," said Ann.

"But I'm a very good truthteller," said Henry. "I want to tell you the truth about me. Without jokes. Or comic overtones. Burn all my bridges as a liar. I'd like you to know me as I know myself. Because we can't start over unless you do. Maybe we can't even then. I may disgust you too much as a man of truth. Or make you see me as an utter fool. Women usually run like mad at the first sign of honesty in a man."

"I don't know," said Ann, "I've never heard any first signs."

"A few," he smiled nervously. "I used to sugar-coat them as generalities. Darling—" he paused. Ann waited. "He *is* suffering from something," she thought.

"I'll ask Elsie to plead my case," Henry said softly. Ann was silent. "I mean my case as a devoted mate. You think she is, don't you?"

"Elsie's my best friend," said Ann, "please don't pick on her."

"I'm not going to. I'm relying on Elsie and her virtues to exonerate me—a little."

"Elsie loathes everything you are and stand for," said Ann.

"Exactly," said Henry, "just as I do—now. I'm dragging Elsie in as a witness to testify about the unimportance of sinning. The unimportance of stray copulation in a well-ordered marriage. Please don't run upstairs." He put a hand on her arm. Ann sat down in her chair again. "Thank you. It's a rather dull story. But psychologically very important . . . to both of us. And it'll give me strength to stick to the truth—all the way. About myself."

"I'll try to listen—without nausea," said Ann.

"It may be a little difficult at first," Henry said. "You remember that hoopla over Sam and his sinful secretary? The Phi Beta from Vassar with skinny legs. And Elsie walking in, unannounced, and finding them industriously coupled on the office couch?"

"I don't want to hear about Mr. Hartnett's sins," said Ann.

"A little patience," Henry smiled. "I enter the picture in a moment. The couch incident, you remember, almost killed poor Elsie. It was the first time she'd ever caught Sam off base. Which shows she's not very fast on her feet. Do you mind a digression? I'd like to throw in a little background material—just to bring you up to date on Elsie and Sam and me."

"So far I can't follow anything you're saying," said Ann. "You were much more lucid as a liar."

"Lying is creation," said Henry, "and fine editing. When you tell truths you're sort of limited as an entertainer."

"Yes, I know," she quoted coolly, "'good husbands are dull ones.'"

"It's about the time Sam and I were in Palm Beach waiting for both of you to join us," said Henry, "and Elsie flew down ahead of you. You had a cold, I think, or something."

"Dentistry," said Ann.

"Sam and I had a hotel suite together," Henry went on, "to save expenses before you ladies arrived. Well, I came back from the beach early one afternoon, and found Sam in the hay with the hotel's public stenographer. I stepped quickly away from the scene of lust into the parlor and the phone rang. It was an alert bellboy notifying us that Mr. Hartnett's wife was on her way upstairs.

"I interrupted Sam and gave him the tidings. He leaped out of bed like a marlin and flew into a bathrobe. We worked in silence. I pulled off my coat and shirt and climbed into the sheets with the public stenographer—an eager but unappetizing type. I lay in my trousers and shoes, only my naked top showing above the sheets. The poor girl was shaking with terror and hanging onto me. She expected a howling wife to come striding in with a shooting iron.

"I was telling her to relax and take it easy when I heard the bedroom door behind me open. I got a peek of Sam pointing out the two nudes in his bed and of Elsie, with a wrath-of-God scowl, absorbing the evidence that exonerated her own husband, and the sweat of lust still on him."

"I don't believe it," said Ann.

"You can ask Elsie."

"I'm sure you were there as described—nude with a pub-

lic stenographer beside you," said Ann, "but I don't believe
the motivation. And innocence. Or anything."

"I swear on my life and yours," said Henry.

"A minor oath," Ann said. She frowned, "I can't imagine
Elsie not telling me."

"She didn't," said Henry, "because I fixed that."

Ann hesitated, and then asked, "How?"

"I consoled her in her great grief over Sam's wickedness
with the Phi Beta."

"What are you trying to tell me?" Ann asked.

"That sin is to be found among the most unsinful," said
Henry, "and that it doesn't change their character. Elsie, for
instance, is still a fine example of ideal American wifeliness."

"My God, Elsie!" Ann looked at him. "You did that to
her?"

"It was a mutual enterprise."

"You went to bed with Elsie," Ann said. "She let you!
Oh, no, I can't believe it of her."

"Yes, you can," said Henry. "It almost happened to you—
a few nights ago. And your virtue is much deeper—and
more complicated than hers."

"Does Sam know?" Ann asked.

"Naturally not."

"How long did your affair last?" Ann's face was pink.

"About two hours," said Henry, "counting both visits."

"If you're lying to me, Henry Lawrence," Ann said, "I'll
never see you or speak to you again."

"I'm too desperate to lie," said Henry. "I want you to

know *me*. Me as I am. No fairy tale husband. But the real and horrid McCoy."

"It makes me feel sick," Ann looked away. She thought, "That foul hypocritical bitch of an Elsie. I wish I could ask him some details." But she remained silent, in deference to the pain in his eyes.

"The reason I want to tell you what I've been," said Henry, "is that I'm a different man now. And can thus afford confession. It won't interfere with any future pleasures—because there won't be any."

"That makes me feel very sad for you," Ann said coolly.

"You'll believe me later," said Henry, "just listen now. The arrest, jail, scandal, pulled me out of something I've been since I can remember. An attitude. A sort of agile impostor. Most sensible men are—for quite a while. Until they get tripped up, emotionally. A man pretends everything including the fact, sometimes, that he's a man."

"That's really evil about Elsie," Ann said. The subject fascinated her more than Henry's generalities.

"It is. It was," Henry said. "I had no more desire to go to bed with her than with a floor lamp. I was able to function only by talking about you—and your superior charms."

"How utterly filthy!"

"Yes," said Henry, "we both seduced Elsie. It was quite evil, as you say. There wasn't even a sexual excuse for the performance. I did it as a gambit—to shut her up about Palm Beach."

"But you hadn't done anything in Palm Beach, you say," Ann looked at him. "Or had you?"

"I hadn't. But the evidence was against me," Henry smiled tensely, "if Elsie took the stand. The only way I could make certain you would believe I'd been moral was to seduce Elsie and line her up as a character witness."

"What a lot of work to go to," Ann kept her voice casual.

"Hardly any work at all," said Henry. He looked at her painfully. "That's why I asked those jealous questions about you and Sam. I had my own data on wifely devotion and chastity."

"And I have mine," said Ann. "The confession over?"

"Just begun."

"There were others?" she hadn't meant to speak the words.

"I was faithful to you for four years," said Henry. "Four lovely years. Then I fell off the fidelity wagon. My first violation was Mrs. Kiley, wife of our best-selling critic."

"How ugly!"

"They were all ugly," Henry said quickly, "including Vangie."

"Oh, no!" Ann shivered, "not that one! She's awful." She recalled the blondined, rawboned, mouth agape, comic-valentine of a siren who was Henry's receptionist. "I don't want to hear any more."

"I've almost run out of material," said Henry. "There were six, counting Elsie. Well, now you've got it all." He stood up and walked the room. "Darling, I'm no Sam Hartnett. I can't shed tears. But I'm sick of what I've been. I'm sick of my godam empty theories. With no home in them. No

151

beliefs I can call me. And I'm sick of playing a sort of bored pagan behind your back. Darling, forgive me."

Ann thought, "That easy? A few words and you're a new man. With a noble heart. A fine set of principles."

"Please," said Henry, "try."

She was silent.

"If you want to go to Bermuda with me for a few months," he smiled, "I'm your fella."

"I can't think of anything I want," said Ann.

"I love you," Henry said. She was silent. "As I used to say in my salad days—shall we go upstairs?"

"No."

"Give me a chance," he said.

She shook her head.

"Sensuality is a good remedy for shock," he said, "draws the blood out of the head."

He waited, and then came to her. He sat on the arm of her chair. "Like Sam," she thought. She looked up at him. Four years of betrayal, lies, mockery smiled back at her, tenderly, wistfully. This deceiver with the hurt eyes was the man she had loved with her soul and body. Then how could she sit like this—with no feeling? No pang of grief, not even resentment. "I'm cold," she thought calmly. A chill was in her belly.

"Darling," he whispered. He kissed her mouth. Suddenly, he was standing in front of her and speaking calmly.

"Do you want a divorce, Ann?"

She started to get up without answering.

"Don't go," he said softly. "I won't touch you. You're

152

like a frozen robin. Even your thighs—ice cold. The way they used to be—before Miami. I'm not an oaf. I understand what I've done. I've shocked you back to frigidity. And it'll probably take some time to—unshock you. Please let me try, though. Nothing but the truth, from here in. First, about Liza. I can't turn my back on her. Except sexually. And romantically."

She listened to him talk on, and her thoughts returned. "He's trying to be truthful about Liza. But it's a truth that applies only to me. He has another set of truths for Liza. He's been two men. And he's trying to get back into one package." She noticed with surprise that there were tears in his eyes, and his voice was wavering. If she reached her hand to him he would start weeping aloud—like Sam. No, not like Sam. Not with fear and self-disgust, but with his need of her and his pain for having hurt her. And his desperate wish to be only one side of himself—the side that would get him into no more trouble.

He was talking about their past, now. The four lovely years. The many lovely years like them still unlived. Why not let him melt the chill in her, she thought.

"I need your help, Ann." He leaned toward her. "Please help me. A man gets scattered alone. Put me together, darling. Not now. But soon. Soon as you unfreeze."

She was silent.

"Liza was a craziness," he said softly, "a sort of climax of my college-boyism. A surviving hobby—like butterfly chasing. Or stamp collecting. Whatever it was, it's dead and gone. You don't have to think of it as still going on.

153

Look, Ann my darling, I'm what you always thought I was. I'm someone with no outside secrets. I'm complete. And yours only. My darling, I need you."

He came to her and knelt in front of her.

"My God," she thought, "he's going to do what Sam did. And I'll react like Elsie."

She stared at his head in her lap.

"Excuse me," Hannah spoke from the door, "the policeman is here again."

Henry stood up quickly. Sergeant Davies walked in.

"Sorry to intrude," he said. "This will just take a minute." His face was expressionless.

"What do you want?" Ann asked.

"I thought Mr. Lawrence might know where Miss King is hiding," said Davies.

"Is she hiding?" Henry asked.

"Do you know where?"

"No," Henry answered. "I went to see her after being released. I waited in her apartment for fifteen minutes. She didn't show up, and I came home."

"Have you heard from her, Mrs. Lawrence?"

"No."

Sergeant Davies looked at the carpet.

"He's half mad," Ann thought. "Liza told the truth about him."

"Miss King is a desperate woman," Davies said. "I don't think either of you realize that."

"Desperate in what way?" Henry asked.

"She's not sane," Davies said.

"Aren't you being a little too personal for a cop?" Henry said. After a pause, Davies answered, "I take it you know about Liza and me."

"You take it right," Henry's voice sharpened.

"Did you help her get away?" Davies asked softly. Henry was silent. "If you did, you're obstructing the law," Davies went on. "She's a murderess. She killed Tom Sovey. She hasn't got a chance to stay under cover. Not Liza." His eyes glared at Henry. "I helped you out, Mr. Lawrence. You might return the favor. Where is she?"

"I told you, I don't know," Henry answered loudly. "Damn it, man, I don't want her running and hiding. I want her to stand up to your godam delusions that she's guilty—and prove what a horse's ass you are in a court of law."

"Excuse me," Hannah said from the doorway. "Phone for you, modom."

An instinct brought Ann to her feet. She knew who it was.

"I'll take it in my room," she said, and looked coldly at the sergeant. "If you want to ask me any more questions, I'll be upstairs."

She walked away slowly but fearfully. He didn't come after her. But he might pick up the phone and listen in. No, not in front of Henry.

In her room, Ann closed the door.

"Hello," she said into the phone.

"It's Liza," the voice said. "I need you. I'm at Sixty-ninth Street and Second Avenue. In a barroom on the corner. Please come."

155

"I'll try. He's here," Ann said.

"Henry?"

"Yes. But I mean the sergeant."

"Frank?"

"Yes. He's looking for you."

"Take my number," Liza gave her a phone number. "Call me if you're held up. I'll wait for you or your call."

Ann hung up and looked in the wall mirror. "I wonder why she called me," she thought, "and trusts me so much? I wonder why I'm going." She saw the pulse moving too quickly under her neck skin. "I've got to go," she thought, "even if it's wrong. Even if she's guilty." She decided against sneaking out of the house the back way. The sergeant would spot her and follow.

She walked down the stairs. The two men were glaring at each other. As she stood in the hall door, Davies said, "If you see her, Mr. Lawrence, give her this message from me—I'm going to make her feel worse than the Princess did."

"Could you be more explicit?" Henry said. "What princess?"

"That was Elsie," Ann smiled at her husband. "She wants to see me about something important. I think it's a Henry Lawrence victory dinner."

"Want me to come along?" Henry asked.

"No, thanks," she said. "I'd rather be alone for a while."

Opening the front door, she heard Sergeant Davies ask, "May I use your phone, Mr. Lawrence?"

"Go right ahead," Henry said.

Ann waited. The living room was silent.

"He's waiting for me to leave," she thought. "Good-by," she called and walked out of the house. She climbed casually into her car in the driveway, as if her pulses were not full of panic.

She drove past two drugstores. At the third, a mile from the house, she stopped. Inside its phone booth, she dialed the number Liza had given her. Liza answered.

"Hello, this is Ann."

"I was waiting in the booth here," said Liza. "I felt you'd call."

"I think your sergeant friend caught on," said Ann, "and knows I'm going to you. Was he ever with you in that barroom?"

"Yes. We used to come here often!"

"Then he'll head for it even if he loses me," said Ann. "You'd better go some place else."

"I will," said Liza. "I'll be in the park across the street from the Doctors Hospital. You know the place, Ann?"

"Yes."

"I'll watch for you," said Liza.

Ann hung up.

Outside, she looked up and down the street. The thought of the blond sergeant shocked her, as if he were some ogre with magic powers. He had read her mind as she stood in the hall door talking to Henry. She had expected Henry to know she was lying about Elsie—and guess Liza. But not the thick handed sergeant. He would know she was heading for the George Washington Bridge. There was no other

way into New York. Except the Tappanzee Bridge, and
that would mean a twenty-mile detour. Ann decided on the
detour. Liza would know she was coming. And wait.

Ann circled Englewood on a back road and headed north-
ward. She thought of Liza with two different sets of words.
"She's guilty. She's planning to use me in some way. Blackmail, perhaps. She's a murderess. She'll do anything to get
off, and to escape." And other words, "Poor Liza. That
damned policeman's in this deep. She's lied to me about
him. Because she's scared of him. All that business of wanting to die. That's fear. Oh, yes," she tried to stop thinking,
"I used to be afraid. And want to die."

Capricious memories came to her. About her parents.
Her tall, humorous father whom she had hated from in-
fancy to adolescence. And he had hated her. He had
knocked her down several times—in her early teens. But
that couldn't be true, she thought. "I used to pretend he
had. And tell mother." The word "mother" hurt her heart
delicately, as it always had since she could remember. Once
when she was nine, her mother had insisted on going to an
afternoon bridge party. Ann remembered screaming for
her mother to stay in the house and play with her. A few
minutes later she had flung herself to the ground as her
mother was taking the car out of the driveway. She had
lain face down in the dirt, waiting for her mother to run
over her in the car—or stop the car and stay home with her.
This was a true memory, but she couldn't remember the
sequel. Had her mother remained home and played with
her? There was no way of ever finding out, she thought,

158

with tears coming to her. Both parents had been killed in a train crash in Switzerland. If not for her roommate Margo, she might have thrown herself under the wheels of a train when she heard the news.

"I didn't hate him after I grew up," she thought of her tall, humorous father. He used to speak like Henry. Profanely and tenderly and mockingly. "Mother never loved him, poor man," she sighed. "She couldn't bear his touch or kisses. But she must have borne them once. I wasn't delivered by a stork."

Evening had quieted the city when Ann walked from her car toward the river. She saw Liza sitting alone on a bench like a spectacular castaway. The river behind her was full of lonely sounds. The blazing city a few miles away was a distant parade.

Ann stood in front of Liza and felt pity. The girl was as inert as a rag doll. A newspaper was on the bench beside her.

"I took the Tappanzee Bridge," Ann said. "I didn't want Davies to spot me."

"He'll find me," said Liza.

Ann sat down beside her, and felt the thrill of strength. Life was something you led on a leash. It walked beside you.

"What's more, I don't care if he finds me," said Liza "—not much. I'd just as soon have it over."

"Don't talk like a fool," said Ann.

Liza's eyes, large and sullen, looked at her. "I shouldn't have dragged you into this, Ann."

"You haven't dragged me into anything," said Ann.

"I'm no good for anyone," Liza said. "I hurt everybody who comes near me. I was going to ask you for some money to get out of town. I didn't dare go to the café or my apartment. I ran as soon as I read in the paper that I was 'it.' Soon as I read it, I knew the whole score."

Liza smiled faintly. Ann glimpsed the strong teeth and patted her arm. "She's in a panic," Ann thought, and said aloud, "I love the river when it gets dark. You can see the world long ago. Before there were people."

"Must have been a wonderful place," Liza said. "Imagine —no people. Nobody hating anybody."

"Just a river flowing," said Ann. "And some birds sitting on it. You're trembling, Liza."

"Yes, I'm trembling," Liza said, "but I'm not running away. I'll stick and let Frankie do his stuff."

"He'll do nothing," Ann said. "All we have to do is keep our heads—till tomorrow. Then the gentlemen can take over."

She opened her purse and removed the pasted-together Sovey letter.

"I found this in your bathroom," she said, "in the laundry bag."

Liza glanced at the envelope and looked at Ann intently. "Snooping, eh?" Ann was silent. A tension left Liza. She smiled. "You were working to save Henry. That it?" Ann nodded. "Do you love him?"

"I don't know any more," said Ann.

Liza looked gay and eager. "I know what you mean about not knowing," she said. "It's like a nosebleed. You don't know when it starts. Or stops." She leaned her head against Ann's hair. "You're very cute, Ann. Playing detective with that jerk Sam. And being a jerk, he thought it was for real, I suppose." She chuckled. "And I told Henry what a hot time you were having with your Sammy. It must have knocked the wind out of Henry. I love it." She laughed aloud. "You know, honey, I never quite believed it. There was something unnatural about you going for that kind of guy."

Ann thought, "She's lost all interest in Henry." She added with a shiver, "Even more than I have."

"What changed your mind about me being the murderer," asked Liza, "or have you?"

"Yes, I have," said Ann, "I don't think I ever really believed you did it. I was just trying to convince myself."

"For Henry's sake. To get him out." Liza stared at her. "I'll be damned. What an act! All for Henry."

Ann ignored the Henry side. "Even after I found my big clue, Sovey's letter, I couldn't believe in your having done it. You're too straightforward to kill anybody. And too childlike."

"I'm childlike," Liza repeated softly.

"Good lord, yes," said Ann.

"Childlike to me means only one thing," Liza said, "nobody loves you and it's cold in the room. Only four walls at night to put you to sleep. Childlike." She smiled at Ann.

161

"That's why I keep wanting to die. Whenever I look back and see that kid called Liza."

Ann patted Liza's arm and recited one of Henry's mocking speeches, "There, there, little girl—don't cry. I knew your father. We were pals in the Yukon."

It was enjoyable, sitting beside a frightened girl, giving her strength to smile, watching the river and the darkening night.

"She needs me," Ann thought. "It's amazing that I don't hate her. I guess I'm not a wife any more." A small pinch of pain denied this. But it was a faraway pinch. It made her strength feel more pleasant. Liza's hand came timidly around her fingers. It closed and remained motionless and moist. Liza's face was also motionless. Ann felt startled.

"What's on your mind?" she asked.

"Nothing."

"Something's upsetting you. I can feel it."

"No, nothing," the husky voice was stubborn.

"You're watching for something," said Ann. "Ever since I sat down. You've been waiting and looking. What is it, Liza?"

"Nothing that I can think of."

Ann thought, "Damn her. Like a sulky child. Why does she keep on lying to me—about one thing or another?"

"You can trust me," she said aloud.

"I know. You didn't hand in the letter."

Ann smiled, "All right, Miss King, if you won't talk, you won't talk. I'll have to handle it myself. I'll get a private detective tomorrow to start clearing up the Tom Sovey mystery. It shouldn't be difficult. Henry gave Sovey a hundred dollars in that saloon. Someone saw Sovey get the money and held him up later."

"Tom wasn't robbed," said Liza, "he blew the hundred in for dope."

"The robber didn't know that," said Ann.

Liza looked away. "I oughtn't to tell you. Because I don't want you to get involved, Ann. I really don't, darling." Her hand tightened around Ann's fingers. "Go away, Ann," she whispered. "Quick. Before something happens. Good-by. Go away, please."

The hand left her fingers. Ann looked at the twisted face. "What is it, Liza?"

"I know who killed Tom Sovey," Liza said. Ann was silent. She knew, too. "And he's coming to kill me. Soon," Liza added.

"Frank Davies," said Ann.

Liza nodded. She moistened her heavy lips with her tongue.

"I can feel him. Like I can feel that river," Liza's bosom rose and fell. "Oh, God, I'm so scared I want to jump in. And get it over with."

"Stop it, Liza!"

"He's going to kill me."

Ann's hand touched the back of Liza's neck under her warm hair. "Please don't," she said, "don't be afraid of him."

"I'm all right now," Liza said softly. "It just hit me all of a sudden."

Liza lifted Ann's hand to her lips and kissed it. The kiss

left a large red print in her palm. Ann closed her fingers over it.

"I'll tell you about it," said Liza, "why he killed Tom. And why I'm next." Her voice was calm and even amused. "Like Henry's," Ann thought, "the voice that stays outside of everything." Her hand opened. In the street light, she saw the red mouth print on her palm. "It's still there," she thought, "a woman's rouge." She closed her hand again to keep from staring at it.

"I married Tom Sovey," said Liza, "because he was ashamed to continue taking money from me as my sweetie. Men and their damned egos! They're really something. There was also another reason why I married him. He was impotent. It's a laugh. But impotent men always go for me. And vice versa." The voice grew mocking. "No offense, Ann. Henry was the exception." She sighed. "So I married Tom and he was able to live off me without his pride being wounded."

"No sex at all?" asked Ann.

"A different kind of sex than you know," said Liza, "or Henry knows."

"It sounds very special," Ann said.

"He'd hold me in his arms at night when I felt lonely and cried. He'd be full of hop and he'd hold me gently as if I was three years old and recite poetry. He had a fine actor's voice. And he always talked in a whisper when he was hopped."

"Davies killed him because he was jealous of him," Ann said, "is that it?"

"No," Liza said, "they were pals. Frankie got him all the dope he needed, free. And Tom paid off by telling Frankie all about me. Everything. All the details. Men who called up. What perfumes I used. How I felt when Tom held me. Was my skin warm or cold. What I said when I cried. Tom told me all about his talks with Frankie. It made me feel funny. But I didn't mind. Then the boys broke up. I don't know why. But Frankie gave Tom the brush-off. No more free dope. And no explanations. He just said one day, "The hell with you. Get lost," and my troubles began. Tom needed more and more money for his dope. I got sore and finally kicked him out. A few months before Henry. I kicked him out and kept him out."

"But he came back," Ann said.

"A month ago," said Liza, "and it was a different Tom Sovey. No gentleman actor spouting poetry. But a real mean bastard yelling for dough. And screwy as hell. Henry heard him talking to me on the phone. You can imagine how I had to lie."

"About what?"

"About his being my husband."

"Why?"

"I don't know. I've always got to lie about things. But I got tired of lying and let Henry trip me up. I told him Tom was still my husband. My God—what a scene! All right for him to be married. But for me—it just showed what an unprincipled bum I was." Liza smiled vaguely. "I guess he was right. Oh, God, I'm such a mess. Such a lousy mess. I'd like to jump into that river. And would I jump hard!"

"Stop it," Ann said.

"It comes over me in a wave," said Liza. "Frankie Davies. I can feel him looking for me. Coming for me. Getting me."

"What a crybaby you are," said Ann.

"On account I used to be an orphan," Liza sneered. "It puts the finger on you. On me and Frankie."

She became silent and Ann thought, "I'm holding her together. She'd go to pieces without me."

"After Henry gave Tom the hundred," said Liza, "Tom bought his hop and came to my place. And there was something more than dope in him. He started his godam junkie whispering that he was still my husband and wasn't going to let me break up the sanctity of another man's marriage. But that was only half of it. First, before straightening my life out, the poor junkie was going to put Sergeant Davies in his proper place. Frankie was coming up for his first big promotion to lieutenant. All Tom had to do was to tell them who and what Frankie was—a dope pusher and whore peddler. And that was curtains for Frankie-boy. Out of the department and into jail. I said to him, 'Leave Frankie alone. You got enough troubles.' And he answers, 'I'm not leaving anybody alone, including you. I'm going to get what's coming to me.' And he did."

"You're just guessing," Ann said, "that he found Frank Davies and tried to blackmail him."

"I'm not guessing," Liza said. "I know from what the papers said. About those two girl neighbors of mine who claimed they heard me and Sovey screaming at each other, that I was a home-wrecker, and that I'd break his neck if

166

he didn't leave me alone. You read that deal, didn't you?"

"Yes. Were they lying?"

"No," Liza said. "All those things were said, almost exactly as in the paper. But Tom Sovey was whispering. And I was talking soft. Not to have anyone hear me."

"Then somebody wire-tapped your apartment, or whatever they call it."

"No," said Liza, "a wire tap would have had the talk about his going off after Frank Davies. It wasn't a tap. Tom met Frankie and reported it all to Frankie. Like he used to do. And he started laying down the law to Frankie. Frankie knows hoppies inside out. His mother taught him. He knew he was done for if Tom kept going. He killed him. And he fixed up those two girls across the hall with Tom's story to tell. They're whores out of his stable, probably. He must have put them there to take Tom's place as spies on me."

"What made him change his mind about pinning the killing on Henry?" Ann asked.

"Two things," Liza said. "He must have been hopped up when he killed Tom. He's always high at night—after hours. When he sobered up he realized Henry wasn't a good suspect. He found out Henry was home with you, when Tom was still alive. And that I talked to Henry while Sovey was with me. So that let Henry out. Two of us could say where he was around the time Tom got killed." She stopped and shivered. "Oh, is somebody walking on my grave! Feel." She held out her forearm. "My skin's jumping."

Ann touched the skin. It was hot as if with fever.

"You said two things," Ann patted the warm arm. "What's the other?"

"Frankie's love for me is the other," Liza said. "It came back to him. It drove him crazy again. That's the kind of girl I am—I drive men crazy by spitting on them like a witch. It must have come back in his belly and started him howling for me at night. I knew it when he held my arm in the jail. I knew it and I felt good, like a fool. I was glad he was howling again. But now, I feel sorry for both of us."

"It's quite a story," Ann said, "and it will be easy to prove. I'll give Henry and Sam all the details tomorrow at noon. They'll prove it."

"They won't," Liza said.

"Don't be childish," Ann said. "Davies can't possibly cover up all he's done."

"He isn't going to try covering up anything," Liza said. "He's let go. He just wants me. He's only figuring it as far as me."

Ann held her arm.

"I knew he'd go over the edge sometime," Liza said. "I remember his eyes—when he started howling for me. It was like looking into hell. That's where he is now. He'll take me with him."

"No, Liza," Ann squeezed the arm. "I'm with you."

"That helps," Liza smiled.

"Sergeant Davies is a revolting and lunatic policeman," said Ann. "I loathed him on sight, as I told you. His thick hands. And that baritone purr. But he's only one man. And his goose is cooked."

168

"Maybe," Liza sighed, "with you helping, I'm not so afraid."

"I can't understand how you could start with such a rotten fellow?"

"I could start with almost anybody who asked for me," Liza answered, "because it didn't mean anything. And it used to make me feel strong."

Ann was glad the subject had veered. "Going to bed with men you didn't care about. That made you feel strong?"

"Yes. I'd lie listening to their passion and watching them grind their teeth. And feel superior. Because I was calm. Untouched. A man falling apart with passion was fun to watch."

"Henry, too?"

Liza looked at her in silence. "What a relief to get back on Topic A. But I don't want to hurt you, Ann."

"You won't."

"Henry knew I was a fake. The first night, he spotted my phony act of passion. When I got out of the bed to go to the bathroom, I pretended to be sexually exhausted. I said, 'I'm so weak, I can hardly walk.' And he laughed like hell. After that there wasn't much hanky-panky. Just talk. I'd take the witness stand and Henry would sail in like a district attorney."

"Didn't he ever make you feel?"

"Sort of," Liza sighed. "But it was hardly worth the effort. What he did chiefly was give me a headache." She smiled at Ann. "I'm lying," she went on. "He didn't make me feel. No man can. I lied to you about Frankie making

169

me feel. God damn me, I was always a dead ass. A dead ass. I'm a damned freak. Built for men. Every inch of me. They go crazy when they hold me, naked or dressed. And me! A lot of foam rubber without a nerve ending. Dead. Dead. Somebody put a curse on me when I was born."

Ann thought, "It may be true." But she felt wary. Liza's confession pleased her too much.

"I tried my damndest with Henry," said Liza, "like a one-armed man trying to learn to play the fiddle. It would work for a few minutes until he began to feel. Then I'd go dead again. And lie there with a secret grin. God knows about what!"

"You felt superior," Ann reminded her.

"Like pansies feel superior," said Liza, "because they can't feel anything else. But the crazy part of it was that I wanted Henry. It got so I had to have him around to holler at me. I felt he was curing me of something. And," she looked boldly at Ann, "I used to make him talk about you."

"Me!"

"Yes, describe you. Your sex habits, quirks. All your tricks—before he supposedly ditched your bed."

"For God's sake," Ann began. She stopped. She remembered Henry's detailed recitations of her predecessors' sexualities. They had included everything.

"I know you," Liza said softly. "That's why I'd like you to know me."

"Sounds fair enough," Ann used her suburbia voice.

"Don't be sore," said Liza.

Ann thought, "How can she imagine I'm a Lesbian like

she is when she knows all those things." She shuddered at the pictures of herself in Liza's head. "Unless she's lying again. But she isn't. That's Henry's forte—past-tense pornography. But how can she think I'm queer, then?" A curious answer came, "Because all women are queer."

Ann looked at the vivid face beside her. She took Liza's hand. "You're shivering," she said. "Frightened again?"

"No," Liza said. "I was just trying to think straight about Henry. It's hard for me to think straight. I go off automatically into lies."

"The way a child does," said Ann. "Reality and make-believe are the same to a child."

"I'm some baby," Liza smiled. Her hand tightened slowly on Ann's. "The chief thing about Henry was that he wanted all my secrets. And every time I'd try to tell him one, he'd call me a liar. And twist my words around till I thought I'd go nuts."

"But you were lying to him, weren't you?" Ann asked.

"All the time," said Liza. "It was a game. A crazy game. I wanted him to find me but I kept hiding more and more from him. I never told him anything real. I mean actually truthful. I'd make up dirty confessions to hide the truth behind. Do you know what I mean?"

"Sort of," Ann said. "By confessing things that never happened, you could always deny them—and remain innocent. And he would never have anything on you, really."

"Something like that," said Liza. "Oh, it's wonderful to talk to you. I feel alive, all over. Oh, darling." She raised Ann's hand and kissed it eagerly.

"I'm glad you feel human again," Ann said. She smiled at her reddened hand, and thought, "Evidence of some phantom crime."

"I've almost forgotten about Sergeant Dracula," said Liza. "Oh, no, I feel more than that. I'm crazy about you. You've given me back—everything."

It was dark. They stood up. Ann thought, "People get arrested for this sort of thing," and resisted an urge to embrace the grateful girl.

"I'll send Henry a telegram," Ann said. Liza's hand clung to hers as they walked. "So he won't imagine I've drowned myself with a broken heart."

"Don't go home," Liza said huskily.

"I won't leave you alone," Ann smiled. "I know a nice hotel on West Seventy-second Street. Henry and I went there once—for some reason."

She smiled at the memory—a walk in a spring city night and a quick hunt for a Venus grotto.

A silent Liza beside her, she toured the streets until a Western Union office appeared.

"I'll be out in a minute," Ann said.

"No, I'm going in with you."

"You're like some helpless, drooling wife," Ann laughed. "I never could have imagined it."

They were in the office. Ann wrote out a telegram: "Will call on you tomorrow at your office around eleven. Important." She signed it, "Ann."

"It's a perfect telegram," Liza smiled. "It'll drive him crazy."

172

Ann felt happy, as if she were suddenly without problems or memories. She felt buoyant with youth, the way she used to feel while walking with Margo.

"A deceived wife has a legal right to drive her husband crazy," said Ann. Liza laughed, and Ann joined her laughing.

They walked in the street to Ann's car. Ann drove off.

"Do you want to go to a movie, Liza?"

"I hate movies," Liza said.

"Why?"

"Do you want to hear something funny?" Liza asked. Ann nodded. "When I'm watching a movie, I never look at the men's faces on the screen. I always look at their bodies." She grinned.

"That's insanity," Ann said. "You're really insane." Liza nodded solemnly. "But why?" Ann asked. "If you hate the male so much, why stare at his body?"

"I don't know, darling," Liza said. "I just stare. As if—as if I was trying to find something. Anyway, it ruins a movie."

"Yes, one misses a lot concentrating on what makes a man a—well—a male." She laughed at her joke.

"I can't get over," Liza said, "what a jerk I was—even half falling for you and that Sam deal."

"I almost half fell for it," Ann smiled.

"Don't try to pretend," Liza said. "You wouldn't go to bed with a fool like that in a thousand years."

"I tell you I almost did," said Ann, happily.

"There's no such thing as 'almost,'" said Liza.

173

"In my circle, 'almost' is the password," said Ann. "Do you mind telling me one thing?"

"Anything, Ann."

"About that row you had with Henry. That ended in your nosebleed. And his bloodstained muffler."

"Yes, that's right," Liza said.

"You were angry because Henry had to leave and go home to me?"

"Did Henry tell you that, Ann?"

"No. Sam told me."

"It's a damn lie," Liza said. "I was trying to chase him out of the apartment. Because he kept telling me I was a Lesbian who would take on any man, including Tom Sovey, because I had no sensual compass to guide me."

"Sounds involved," Ann smiled.

"Your husband," said Liza, "is the most pretzel-brained torturer that ever wore pants."

Both women laughed. Liza said abruptly, "Turn the corner."

"What is it?"

"A police car," said Liza.

"Sergeant Davies isn't riding up and down a thousand New York streets looking for you," Ann said. "Be sensible." But she turned the corner. The red winking light of the police prowl car was lost. They drove in silence.

"I believe her," Ann thought. "I believe everything she tells me. And it may all be lies. At least half lies. Especially about that sergeant. She lied originally about him. Why not again? She may be trying to win me," Ann smiled at

174

the verb, "by playing the frightened little child. But it doesn't matter since I don't intend to be 'won.'"

Her thought turned to Henry. "It sounds true about Henry. Of course it's true about his third degree tactics. He used to grill me—before Miami. Till he found out I was without previous sin. Or color. Or anything."

She looked carefully into the past as one might feel the edge of a blade. It made no cut in her. "I wonder if it'll come back." She meant the pain. "Yes, I'll probably start suffering later—in his presence. It takes two to suffer correctly."

She thought of Liza's sex confession—her not feeling. What an idiot Henry was, with all his Grand Inquisitor suspicions. Wasting his passion on a rubber woman. A thought surprised her, "It must be a lot of fun to fool a man like that."

The Montgomery Hotel was an old-fashioned roost for unwanted parents, widows and retired keptees. Its lobby was as unromantic as a dentist's waiting room. In fact, there was no lobby. You entered and went to a glass-caged desk at the right. Elderly, overrouged women, and heavy-faced, expressionless men kept emerging from the three elevators and taking ten steps to the swinging street doors.

"I want a suite," said Ann to the desk clerk, "for two of us—my sister and me."

The clerk nodded and turned a register toward her.

"I'll sign for both," said Ann. She signed Ann and Margo Marcher—her maiden name.

"Any bags?" asked the clerk.

175

"We'll pay in advance," said Ann. "Our bags will be here tomorrow."

The clerk said twenty dollars.

During the transaction, a man stood watching the two beauties who had inexplicably entered the dreary hotel. He looked more intently at Liza. Ann noticed him—a fat, short, heavily jowled creature like some underworld comedian.

"Have you room service?" she asked.

"Until nine o'clock, Miss Marcher," the clerk said. He handed her a key.

"Number thirty-three," he said.

Thirty-three was a two-room suite with a cubicle kitchen. The lights revealed a set of stiff green parlor furniture, not too soiled, and three framed reproductions on the walls of British nobility portraits. The bedroom was small and held a chair, a dresser and a large double bed.

"I'll order up some food," said Ann.

"I'm not hungry."

"You've got to eat," Ann was firm. "We have a big day tomorrow."

"I seldom eat," said Liza. "I don't like food."

"Frigidity pattern," Ann thought, "thwart all apertures."

"I want you to eat," she said, "please."

Liza smiled, "You're a real section-gang boss, aren't you?"

"I'm sorry."

"No, I like it," said Liza.

They went into the parlor. Liza stood looking out of the window.

"You belong in a palace," said Ann, "not in a run-down family hotel."

"Do I?"

"Yes," Ann smiled, "the imperious chatelaine in a sweeping purple robe with a wide gold belt."

"How about some sapphires?" Liza smiled back.

"I was going to give you a diamond choker," said Ann at the phone. She called room service and ordered two steaks and a bottle of wine. "But send up two Martinis first."

"Was Sam the only man you almost went to bed with since Henry?" Liza asked.

"Since and before," said Ann.

"Imagine that," Liza smiled, "the perfect wife."

"Virtue's no virtue," Ann said, "when you've got nothing else."

"Don't get so deep," said Liza.

"I mean, I never wanted any man. Not even Henry. But he cured me of my negativism. And sort of invented my glands." Ann smiled. "I was so in love with him, I felt as if I were breathing him instead of air."

"I hate to have busted that up," said Liza.

"You didn't. He did," Ann said. "Besides, who knows what's busted up. You can hate and loathe a man and still love him with all your insides."

"I acted that way," said Liza. "Acting can be pretty real. You can almost convince yourself it's *not* acting."

"Maybe it wasn't," Ann said.

"No, it was all phony," Liza sighed. "When you have no sex for a man, you have no heart, either. It's all put-onski.

Except the getting angry. I couldn't love Henry, but I sure could get sore at him. And it almost seemed the same."

"It's a little hard to love a man," said Ann, "who has to dash off every evening to embrace his wife."

"Was he doing that?"

"You provided me with a second honeymoon," Ann said. She thought, happily, "It's fun being cruel to her, poor thing."

Liza sighed, "I can see why he gave me all that godam talk. He had nothing else to give me." She laughed. "And they call that a love affair—two people conning each other like a couple of crooks."

The doorbell rang. An elderly, bald waiter with a tray of four Martinis appeared.

"I only ordered two," Ann said, "but never mind." She signed the check. The waiter looked at the two women with eager, watery eyes.

"If you want good service, ask for August," he said.

"Thank you, August," Ann said. August bowed and left.

Examining the room casually, Ann thought, "I must be crazy to feel so good. It's like feeling strong instead of weak. And Liza isn't scared any more. She's forgotten about Frankie. About everything, except me." She sipped her cocktail. The room was garish. Its many lamps seemed to advertise inhospitality. "But it's charming," Ann thought. "I feel at home. As I used to with Margo in that dreary dormitory room. It was ours. There were no lies in it, no secrets or malice. Just us—two completely visible human beings." She smiled. "Liza's like that—visible. She's really beautiful, and

178

mystic. There's something mystic in her face that makes her exciting. Because she doesn't know what it is, herself. It's fun here."

Liza sipped her drink. She sat looking almost sullenly at her companion. She watched her examine the portrait reproductions on the wall, watched her cross her legs as she sat down, watched her high instep point the toe of its slipper at the floor.

"You're a sweet girl," said Ann.

"I can't talk," said Liza softly, "I'm afraid to talk to you."

"Don't be frightened," Ann said.

Liza closed her eyes. Her head tilted as if she were going to faint. "Oh, I can't stand it," her voice continued softly, "it's like I was falling off a roof."

Ann leaned over and placed her palm gently against the girl's cheek.

"Don't act, darling," Ann smiled. Liza's eyes opened. Ann looked into them. They were a deepened blue, like mysterious corridors that beckoned. Ann held herself back from the staring blue eyes and thought, "My God, it's like being suffocated."

She stood up.

"I'm going to open a window," she said, and was startled to hear her voice whispering.

Henry Lawrence sat looking at the Hartnetts and wishing they would get the hell out. Ann's telegram was in his pocket. Its brief sentence, read an hour ago, still depressed him. The sentence said he had lost something—an ascendancy. The eight years of being the dominant and desired one were out of existence. He wished his two friends would stop hovering around him and stop enjoying his disaster.

He thought, as Elsie chattered, "It's not malice or gloating. It's just a sort of human enthusiasm for disaster." He recalled a Bret Harte western story about a flood. Harte wrote, "The editor of the Boom Town paper observed with pensive pride 'an area greater than the State of Rhode Island is now under water.'" Sam and Elsie were a pair of such editors.

"You mustn't expect poor Ann to forgive you for some time," said Elsie. "If it were I—" she looked coldly at Sam.

"You're a bitch and Ann isn't," said Henry. Sam frowned but Elsie smiled.

"Dear me," she said, "am I really a bitch?"

"The worst," said Henry, "almost as big a one as Sam deserves."

"Let's leave Sam out of this, shall we?" said Elsie. "Imagine what *you* deserve!"

Henry lit his pipe and thought, "Sweet God, she's flirting with me. What an ogress!"

"How about we go home, before the conversation gets personal," said Sam. "I'm really bushed." He sighed. "It's been a long day, ladies and gentlemen."

"It sure has," Henry yawned. "I bid you both good night and sweet dreams."

"You run along, Sam," Elsie said, "and go to bed. I'll wait

a little longer for Ann. She's going to need me when she comes home."

"Nobody needs you, Elsie," Henry said, "beat it."

"Absolutely not," said Elsie. "If you don't want me to wait inside, I'll wait on the steps."

"Don't stay too long," Sam stood up. "You're pretty tired yourself, darling."

"I'll stretch out on the couch," said Elsie.

Henry thought, "I've got to get out of this."

"I'll take a drink and run," said Sam. "I think it'll be better for everybody if Elsie were here when Ann comes in. Just one for the road," and he fixed a highball.

As if unable to wait for this promised disappearance, Elsie stretched out on the oversized couch near the fireplace.

"Want one, Henry?" Sam asked.

"No, thanks," Henry said, and looked at the suddenly lewd couch. Elsie's air of hauteur was still in her face, but her soft middle rose and fell.

"No, I don't want her," Henry thought. "I told Ann the truth. I've changed." But he continued to watch Elsie's deep breathing and Sam's slow drinking as if some sort of a race were going on.

"I'll tell her the truth about Sam and Ann," Henry smiled inwardly, "that'll get me out of danger." But he said nothing. His vows to Ann were in his head as if they were the complete character of Henry Lawrence. He was what he had vowed to be. But he knew with a sort of foolish disgust that when Sam left the house, Henry Lawrence and all his vows would circle the room for a few moments and come to roost on the couch, alongside Elsie.

"I just hope," Elsie said, "that all this has made you realize what Ann means to you. And how wonderful she is."

"I've always known that," Henry said.

"Then how could you take up with that horrible girl?" Elsie demanded righteously.

"Ask Sam," Henry sneered. He thought morosely, "Look at her wiggling at me, right under her husband's nose. And under her own godam righteous nose. Is it hypocrisy or schizophrenia? Or have women got two brains—an upper and a lower?" He sighed. "And that stupid Sam is going to leave us alone. She's thrown such cat fits over his sins that he thinks she's the voice of God. And that if any man put a hand on her, she'd strike him with lightning."

"Poor Henry," Elsie said, "I shouldn't feel the least sympathy for you, but I do."

"I'm sorry to hear that," said Henry, and he was. The sound of sympathy brought a weakness into him. Tears started in his throat. Elsie chattered on, and Henry thought, "Ann is the only decent woman I've ever known. I can't stand the possibility of her not being Ann any more. I don't want anything or anyone but Ann. It wasn't sex she gave me, it was virtue. I need her virtue. It makes life clean."

He knew he had to stop thinking in this fashion or he would start to weep. He grinned and began to talk brightly to Sam whose highball was half gone.

"I hope that as the next mayor of Englewood you won't

feel it your duty to ban any of my novels from being sold in our pious town."

"Have you gone in for publishing dirty books?" Sam asked with sleepy interest.

"Only three on our fall list," Henry said, "one featuring in splendid detail the rape of a married woman by two house burglars. The second offers an unexpected attack on a nineteen-year-old virgin by her male guardian. However, our big seller will be our third. Its hero—a young priest —lures a Marine into a theater toilet during a performance. And unnatural lust is served to the distant applause of the upstairs audience."

"For God's sake, you're kidding!" said Sam.

"I can see you're not up on modern literature," Henry said. "We have made great strides since the days of the asterisks."

"How do you account for those kinds of books selling?" Sam asked.

"Our country is obviously specializing in masturbation," said Henry. "Have another drink, Sam."

"I shouldn't," Sam started pouring one.

"You certainly shouldn't," Elsie said firmly from the couch. She had removed her slippers and was flexing her feet coyly. "Winking at me with her toes," Henry thought, and repeated, "I don't want her. I don't want her." Sam, thank God, was more than mouse where his liquor rights were concerned. He was working slowly on his new drink. "I'll get this bitch of an Elsie out," Henry thought. "No evasion. Direct attack."

183

Aloud he said, "Look, Elsie, put your slippers back on your pretty little feet and go home. Ann isn't coming back tonight. I happen to know. Definitely."

"You know nothing," said Elsie calmly. "Go to bed if you wish. I'm staying at my post."

"You can enjoy Ann's tears tomorrow," said Henry. "I'm sure they'll still be flowing."

"Hold it," Sam said. "Elsie is Ann's best friend. And, by God, women feel for each other."

"How right you are, Sam darling," his wife sighed. Henry poured himself a large drink. "That silly Elsie excites me," he thought. He smiled at her and asked, "Tell me, Elsie, are you really opposed to sinfulness as a whole, or just to Sam sinning?"

"Sinfulness isn't as bad as deceit," Elsie answered.

"I know," said Henry, "being found out is unforgivable. It frightens all the secret sinners. And brings them down on you."

"Please, it's pretty late," said Sam, "let's not get personal."

"Good idea," said Henry, "continued tomorrow morning." He rose to refill his glass, thinking, "I ought to read her Ann's telegram. She'd have to go, then." But he felt ashamed to read it. He sighed, miserably. It wasn't shame, alone. He was giving the other side of him a small break—the side that was stimulated by Elsie. What a crooked thing the male soul was.

Aloud, Henry said, his voice touched with anger, "Damn

184

it, I haven't hurt Ann by my sins. I've hurt myself. I've destroyed myself in her eyes. She's the same. I'm not."

"I'm glad you feel some remorse, at least," Elsie said.

"If only wives were content with a little remorse," Henry said. "But no! You ladies always yell for John's head."

"John's head?" Elsie repeated.

"John the Baptist," said Henry, "your favorite scene, isn't it? 'Bring me his head on a platter.' 'He's betrayed me.' Meaning he's stopped lying. Fidelity is as big a lie as Jonah and his whale. Nobody swallows it. But everybody pretends to believe in it."

Henry finished his drink and glared at Sam.

"How would you feel if Ann were unfaithful?" Elsie demanded. "I'll bet you'd sing another tune."

"A wife who doesn't betray a husband at least once makes a happy marriage impossible," Henry said. "That's Ann's chief flaw as a mate. I have to pay for her chastity with coin I haven't got—my chastity." His heart hurt at the thought of Ann's nudity in another's arms. Her virtue gone! God God, how could he live in that ruined world? Ann's nudity and Elsie's nudity seemed to merge in his mind, helped by the liquor he had swallowed. He sneered at this Elsie-Ann and asked, "How many men have you dragged into your bed since snaring Sam?"

"None, Mr. Henry Lawrence!"

"As I suspected," Henry said, "it's the cross every husband has to bear—the faithful wife."

"Stop posing," said Elsie, "you'd be devastated if Ann ever betrayed you!"

"No," Henry's mind answered happily, as his heart winced at the news, "it would add a sense of proportion to her wifely attitudes. She wouldn't be making mountains out of *mons Veneris.*"

"I'm going," said Sam. "It's late, and I never like this sort of talk."

"Yes," Henry said, "it's dangerous to talk honestly in front of a wife."

"They take advantage of any opening for cross-examination," said Sam.

"You wretched turncoat," Elsie said, "you shall pay for that remark." Her voice sounded lewd.

"If she puts you in solitary, Sam," Henry said, "there's always my secretary Vangie. An efficient girl with a touch of nymphomania."

Henry poured another drink, thinking hopefully, "Six drinks and I'm impotent."

"You make me realize," Elsie sighed, "how poor Ann must suffer."

"It's only villains who suffer," said Henry. "Good people are too busy sitting in judgment to feel very bad."

"Don't stay too long," Sam said. "Good night, Henry." He leaned over his wife and kissed her. Henry watched him walk out of the room, and started circling away from the couch. "I don't want her," he thought, "she's an overweight hypocrite.

"It's all a pretense," he thought, "all virtue, loyalty, decency, chastity. Even Ann's. It's all masquerade costuming. Damn her soft flesh. She'll be fat as a pig in a few years."

He was still circling. There was no desire in him. He came to the couch and sat down. She looked away from him. A sullenness was in her face.

"I really hate you," said Elsie, "you're so mean. And show-offy. It never occurs to you to talk like a gentleman."

"Not in your presence," Henry said.

"You have fun torturing a woman, don't you?" Elsie sneered.

"Why the hell didn't you go home when I asked you to," Henry demanded, "and avoid being tortured?"

"Because you make me so godam mad that I—"

"That you have to seduce me," Henry finished.

"You're utterly contemptible," Elsie said. "Oh, how I'd like to beat you."

"Not my dish," said Henry. His hand went under her dress.

"Don't," Elsie's mouth was half opened. Her head turned away, as if unable to endure the sight of what was going to happen.

"I told Ann about us," Henry said.

"Oh, no!" Elsie suddenly pushed at the hand holding her under the dress. "You didn't!"

Henry's hand clung. "I did," he said, "but not in full. I said we'd only had two sessions."

"Oh, you dirty bastard!" Elsie moaned, "you torturer!"

"I was too ashamed to tell her about the auto back-seat incident," said Henry, "or the hi-de-ho in the Lockwood's bathroom. I kept you decently on your back in bed."

"I don't believe it," Elsie moaned, "you couldn't be that

187

big a monster. You're just trying to hurt me. Because you're hurt yourself. Ann's hurt you."

"I'm hurt by myself," Henry said. "I'm hurt because I'm as big a fake as you are. As underhanded and weak spined." He stopped.

Their mouths were together. "She kisses like a suction pump," he thought.

The doorbell rang. A second long ring sent Henry to his feet.

"Ann!" Elsie cried. She sat up and in one flow of movement lowered her dress, and put on her slippers. Henry was certain it wasn't Ann, but a great gratitude for whoever it might be filled him.

"Saved by the bell," he grinned at the cliché. "Godam, I'm lucky."

He walked into the hall and opened the door. Sergeant Davies stood in the veranda light.

"You," said Henry. "What do you want?"

"See you a minute," Davies said.

"Come in here," Henry led the way into a small library room off the hallway. He closed the door behind them and looked at the sergeant. His eyes were almost closed. His face was white.

"Is Mrs. Lawrence home?" Davies asked, and sat down.

"No."

"You sure?"

"Very sure," Henry said, and wondered if the sergeant were a drug addict. The whiteness of the face and dryness of the voice, as if all saliva had been burned up in the man—

188

"Don't you ever sleep?" Henry asked. "You seem to keep going day and night."

"I want to close the case," Davies answered. "I'd like to ask Mrs. Lawrence a few questions."

"So would I," said Henry. The man made him nervous. "Look, if I prove to you my wife isn't here, will you answer a few things I want to know?"

"Where is your wife?"

Henry removed the telegram from his pocket and said, "This came two hours ago."

Davies took out a small notebook from his pocket and copied down the Western Union station number on the telegram.

"Then your wife is with Liza," said the sergeant.

"Absolutely not," Henry said. "Who are those two neighbor witnesses who heard Miss King and Sovey quarreling?"

"Their names are in the papers," said Davies.

"Have those two girls been living long at that address?" Henry asked.

"I don't know," the sergeant said. He seemed nearly asleep.

"I intend to find out," said Henry. "I'm absolutely certain Liza didn't kill Sovey."

"Are you?" the sergeant said, softly. He seemed to be listening. "Somebody just left the house, Mr. Lawrence."

"My neighbor, Mrs. Hartnett," said Henry, "her husband is going to defend Liza if you're stupid enough to arrest her."

"If your wife telephones you, I expect you to notify me," said Davies.

"You're out of your mind," Henry glared. "My wife is none of your godam business."

"Your wife left here this afternoon," said Davies, "after receiving a phone call from Miss King. She evaded me by driving to New York via the Tappanzee Bridge."

"Bright gal," Henry said.

"Yes, the police were waiting for her at the George Washington Bridge," Davies said, "and she eluded us."

Henry thought, "There's something screwy about the fellow. He's like somebody under hypnosis."

Aloud, Henry asked, "About those two girl witnesses, Sergeant. Did you try testing how loudly people would have to talk in Miss King's apartment in order to be overheard across the hall?"

"No, I haven't tested that yet," said the sergeant.

Henry studied the policeman while relighting his pipe. Liza's ex-lover. She hadn't lied too much about him when she described him as a smart but subhuman fellow. He thought, "Sovey was a tissue paper man, hop or no hop. This one is a dangerous nut. There's something wild in him as if he's listening to voices. Something's talking to his insides all the time."

Henry stood up.

"I'm staying here," said Davies, "in case Mrs. Lawrence returns."

"I'm not running a flophouse for tired cops," said Henry.

"I'm trying to find Liza King, who is wanted by the

police," the dry, low voice said harshly. "Mrs. Lawrence will be able to tell me where she left her. If Mrs. Lawrence comes in during the next hour."

"You're talking like an idiot!" Henry said. "There's no reason for them to be together. Mrs. Lawrence has her own reasons for staying away from me tonight, as you well know."

"They're together," said the sergeant.

"You're behaving like a man under a hex," said Henry. "I have a notion to call up your station and report your condition." Anger raised his voice. A current from the blond sergeant seemed to enter his senses.

"My condition is excellent," said Davies.

"The hell it is!" Henry said. "I think you're balmy. Either that, or you're full of hop. You're not acting or talking like a policeman. You're after Liza like some hopped-up blood-hound."

"Shut your mouth, Mr. Lawrence," said the sergeant.

"For God's sake," Henry stared at the blond policeman now on his feet. "Look at yourself in that mirror. Smiling. You've kept smiling ever since you came in. Smiling like a loony in a nightmare. Smiling, and screaming inside." He glared at Davies. "What the hell are you carrying a police-man's billy club for," he demanded suddenly, "in your raincoat pocket? Don't try to hide it. You're a sergeant. Sergeants don't carry night sticks."

"I ought to run you in for insulting an officer," Davies' voice was hoarse and calm, "but I've got other things to do."

191

"So have I," said Henry. "I'm notifying your superior officials to take a look at you."

Sergeant Davies walked out of the room. In the hallway, he smiled sleepily at Henry. "Pardon me for the intrusion, Mr. Lawrence," he said. Henry watched him step into the street and drive off in his prowl car.

Henry telephoned the Hartnett house. Sam answered.

"Elsie just got home," he said sleepily, "she's all right."

"I'm not interested in Elsie's condition," Henry said. He related the details of Davies' visit.

"He's a monomaniac on Liza King," Henry said, "he's framing her. Those witnesses across the hall are phonies, Sam."

"I agree with you," Sam said. "I'll get right on it in the morning. First thing."

"We mustn't waste any time," said Henry. "The man's a loony. And dangerous."

"I'll have him up on the carpet first thing," Sam said. "Here, Elsie wants to talk to you."

Henry sighed. Elsie's rapacious sensuality seemed suddenly as revolting as a dentist's drill. But he felt a glow of self-approval at the sound of her voice. He had resisted her, with the aid of Sergeant Davis. How pleasant it felt not to have sinned, entirely.

"Henry darling," Elsie was saying, "promise me if Ann comes home you'll call up. Whatever time it is. I'm really awfully worried about her."

"So am I, Elsie dear," said Henry.

Elsie continued to talk, her breathing growing faster and

her words becoming half sighs. Henry thought of poor, wearied Sam. "A godam lackey to a rapist," he thought, and waited indignantly until Elsie's hoarsened voice said a good night to him.

An hour later, Sergeant Davies entered Liza King's building. He walked up a flight of stairs and rang a doorbell across the hall from Liza's apartment. A thin girl with sickly black eyes opened the door. Davies went in.

He looked around the shabby and disordered living room. A bed was unmade. The floor was littered with newspapers and soiled clothes.

"Where's Greta?" he asked.

"Ain't this room an awful mess?" the girl pulled the clinging wrapper tightly around her. "I can hardly stand it. It's cold, too. A draft keeps comin' out of the walls. You want a boost, Frankie?"

"Where's Greta?" he asked again.

"Oh, Greta," the girl's mouth wavered into a smile. "Oh, she went out. I'll get a boost ready."

"Where'd she go?"

"I'll get the hypo," the girl said. She trembled as she talked. The sergeant grabbed her arms.

"Anybody go into Miss King's apartment, Tin Can?"

"Nobody."

"You're shaking."

"I was waiting to take a boost together. With you. I like it together."

"You going to answer me?" the sergeant asked.

"Answer what, honey?"

"Where'd Greta go?"

"For God's sake, how do I know!" the girl whined.

The sergeant slapped her face. She staggered toward a chair and fell into it.

"Do you know now, Tin Can," his voice was low, "or don't you?"

"Yes, I know, Frankie. I know. I'll get the stuff ready first. The needles are boiled already."

"Sit still. It can wait," Davies looked at her.

"She took her clothes and was goin' back to her roomin' house. I tried to telephone you, Frankie."

"Go on, Tin Can."

"Don't hit me again, please."

"Go on."

"She said she was gettin' from under."

"When?"

"Tonight, I guess."

"Give me her words."

"She said 'I'm goin' to tell the cops what's what.'" She shivered. "I'll get the stuff now."

Sergeant Davies removed the police club from his pocket.

"Don't," the girl whimpered. Her bony face glistened with sweat. Her features twitched. The sergeant stood in silence. He looked vague, like a man who has forgotten something.

194

The girl was unable to move.

"Get it," he said quietly. He put the club in his pocket.

The girl moved away. Her hands shook as she stepped into a closet to change her kimono. A few minutes later she reappeared holding two hypodermic needles.

"You want me to give it to you, Frankie?"

"Go ahead."

She was deft and quick. She sat down sociably in a chair.

"I always enjoy this part most," she said, "when it starts. Lean back in your chair and relax, Frankie."

The sergeant sat stiffly with his eyes looking upward.

"Greta's no good," the girl spoke in a dreamy voice. "She's a scaredy cat. Look, I got seven stitches by my mouth. Can you tell? And fifteen stitches over this eye. When the fella threw me through the window that time. I ain't scared of nothin'! Honest. I'll do anything. We'll have fun. Want to see me do a trick with my eyes?"

"Call up Greta," said Davies.

"You don't want her, I'm here," said the girl.

"Call her up."

"What'll I say to her?"

"Tell her to come over, I'd like to see her."

The girl walked to the phone and dialed a number.

"I wish to speak to Miss Greta Gretz, please. I'll hold the wire."

"How big a boost did you give me, Tin Can?" Davies asked.

"Big," she smiled.

"Too much," he said. "I told you to keep it down."

"Hello," the girl said into the phone. "Greta? He's here. He wants to see you . . . No—I didn't tell nothin'. I said you was goin' to visit your brother-in-law . . . All right— if that's the way you feel, the same to you."

She hung up.

"Frankie," she smiled, "do you know the difference between amnesia and magnesia? Amnesia, you don't know where you're goin'. Magnesia, you know where you're goin'—"

The girl slid out of her kimono as she talked. She lay down on the couch, naked. Her skin was marked with bruises and burns. One of her small breasts was half covered with Band-Aids.

Sergeant Davies' head swayed as he stood up.

"You gave me too big a shot," he said. He stood staring at the room. A red haze covered the walls. The red haze moved over the carpet. It touched his feet. He grinned as the haze crept up his body. He walked out of the room, still smiling.

Greta Gretz listened to footsteps coming up.

"That louse," she muttered, "I should have packed faster."

She closed the suitcase on the lumpy bed and watched the door. It opened and Sergeant Davies came in.

"I wasn't expectin' any company," Greta said.

Davies looked at her heavy knock-kneed legs, her fat, pleated torso and hanging breasts.

"I'm not company," he said.

Greta put on a blue bathrobe.

"You're high," she said. He smiled. "Sit down, for God's sake."

Davies sat down on the bed.

"Come here," he said.

"What for? I'm sick of your kickin' me around."

"You going somewhere, Greta?"

"No, I'm stayin' here."

"Tin Can said you were going to see the police."

"That little skunk."

"Are you?"

"She's crazy."

"Come here," Davies said softly.

"What are you goin' to do?"

"Have some fun."

"I hate you, you dirty bastard."

"I know," he smiled.

"You're a psycho, that's what you are. A stinkin' psycho. I want to puke when I look at you."

"Come here, Greta."

"She had the right name for you—Miss King. Mister Rotten Cork. Did I laugh, when I heard her yellin' at you that time! 'Get out o' here, Mister Rotten Cork, and stay out.' And you stayed out. You were scared of her."

"I like you better," the sergeant smiled. "I said, come here. I'm getting sleepy. Come here, and sit down."

The tall, heavy girl walked slowly to the bed. She looked at him with worried eyes and sat down, obediently.

"I notice you got your teeth in," the sergeant said.

"That's a fine thing to tell a lady," said Greta. "Are you a lovin' type! Oh, mama. What do you want? Listen, I ain't just goin' to sit here while you float around."

"I killed Sovey," said Davies.

"You're tellin' me," said the girl.

"I don't want you to go to the cops with it," Davies said.

"Who's goin' to any cops?"

"Not you," he smiled, "because I need a little time to find her. I don't want a lot of cops stopping me."

"O.K., find her. Who cares? Jeez, how much stuff did you take? Honest, Frankie, you look crazy. You lie down like a good boy. I'll bring you up some coffee."

His arm went around her neck.

"I'm not standin' for any more," said Greta. "Get yourself a new punchin' bag. Hey, let me go. You're hurtin' my neck."

The sergeant tightened his hold. His other hand went quickly to her mouth. His thick fingers pried it open. She tried to scream and bite at his fingers as they tugged the plate out of her upper jaw, leaving it toothless. Her biting became ineffectual. He choked a scream back. Holding the large denture in his fingers, he thrust it into her throat, and pressed it into her windpipe with his finger tips.

Greta groaned and gurgled. Her hands clawed at his face. Her bare feet kicked at him. The groaning and choking subsided. The girl's head sagged. The sergeant let her go slowly. She toppled across the bed. He lifted her legs and straightened her out. He waited and then picked up her wrist. His fingers felt no pulse.

The sergeant stood up. He swayed as he removed his clothes. He lay down in his shorts. His eyes closed. A whimper came from him. "Oh, mama, mama. You with me, mama?"

His glittering eyes opened. Tears were in them. He rubbed the tears out with his knuckles. He looked intently at the dead girl in the blue robe, and suddenly he fell asleep.

*

The waiter pulled the table out of the room, bowing gratefully in the doorway. Ann filled their wine glasses and sat back in her chair, legs extended. She smiled at Liza's moody face with its overexpressive eyes and membranous lips, and wondered if she were as lightheaded from the wine as herself.

"She's beautiful," Ann thought, "but overdone. Like a lithograph. Too much of her shows. Even in her eyes. Her skin is a tiny bit thick. No really delicate side to her. Marriage would turn her into a brood mare. Yes, that's what she is—maternal. The maternal masquerading as a vampire."

An excitement raced her heart. She lowered her eyes and sipped her wine.

"I was trying to remember something," said Liza, "when I was in the orphanage. Around eleven. Oh, yes," she chuckled. "It's a very funny story."

"The superintendent seduced you," said Ann.

"Nothing that grand," Liza said. "Would you like to hear another story?"

"I love your stories," Ann said. She thought, "They *are* wonderful. Better than Henry's. More unexpected." She wondered about Henry. Her telegram would have upset him. He couldn't stand not to be able to talk.

"I was farmed out to a woman named Mrs. Schroeder when I was around eleven," said Liza. "She took in boarders. I washed dishes and made beds. The head boarder was a retired letter carrier, Mr. Curtis. He had the ten-dollar-a-week room. Mrs. Schroeder and Mr. Curtis read the Bible aloud to each other every night. The other boarders always took a powder. One evening before Bible time, Mr. Curtis said to me, 'My room is pretty dusty, little Liza. I'm surprised at you.'

"Mrs. Schroeder said, 'I'm not surprised. Her name ain't little Liza. It's little Lazy. Take a rag and wipe everything clean in Mr. Curtis' room while we read the Bible.'

"I took a rag and was wiping away when Mr. Curtis came in. He grabbed me from behind. I didn't know what the hell he was up to. He got my panties off with me still in the fog. Then he moans, 'little children, oh, little child,' and I thought he was going to cry or pray. Instead he pushes me over and rapes me. It hurt like hell but I was too scared to holler because it was Mr. Curtis, the star boarder.

"Finally he stops mauling and banging me and says, 'get up.' So I got up. He gave me a nickel and said, 'Next week, if you're a good little child, I'll give you two nickels.'

"I went up to my attic room still bleeding and scared to death. I was scared to tell Mrs. Schroeder or anybody. And I was scared of the next week and the two nickels' worth. Well, a few nights later there was a religious revival in a tent in the neighborhood. Mrs. Schroeder and Mr. Curtis went. I tagged along. I stood in the tent listening to the revivalist shouting for sinners to come unto him and give their souls to Jesus and repent their sins. So I finally rushed up to him and threw myself on the ground at his feet and yelled out I was a sinner and how Mr. Curtis had made me sin on the floor. While I was yelling and crying, I felt somebody grab my ear. It was Mrs. Schroeder. She pulled me out of the tent and dragged me off. She kept slapping my face and saying what a dirty little show-off I was. And Mr. Curtis kept throwing in 'yes, we've got a bad little child here.' I ended up on my cot with an earache. I think it's very funny." Liza smiled wistfully into her wineglass.

"It must have given you a trauma toward letter carriers," said Ann. She felt gay, as if a remarkable social event were in progress.

"It didn't endear them to me," Liza smiled. "Do you know what Henry said when he heard that story?"

"Love to hear."

"That it was quite original. Usually the villain in a child rape story was a priest or an uncle. A letter carrier showed a creative mind."

"He didn't believe it?" Ann mocked tenderly.

"Henry believe anything?" Liza chuckled. She was sitting at Ann's feet on the floor. Her hand reached up and

201

found Ann's. "You're better than Henry. You believe my stories. Thank you, darling."

"It's not a matter of believing," said Ann, still with mockery. It was fun to hurt Liza and watch the hunger in her face give place to pain. "It's whether a story is interesting or not that counts. If it's a lie, the *reason* for the lie is also interesting."

"Why in God's name should I tell you lies!"

"You explained that yourself, Liza. That it was automatic. You had to."

"Not to you," Liza raised her face of longing. "Oh, no, no. I want to give you my soul."

"Did you tell Henry about the Princess?" Ann asked.

"God, no," said Liza.

"Was the Princess the first one? Your first Lesbian experience?"

"Yes," Liza answered.

Ann sipped her drink. She knew from the tiny shift of Liza's eyes and the sudden 'note' of sincerity in her answer, and from the brevity of the answer, that this was a lie from Liza. There had been women before the Princess. Ann felt happily superior to Henry, Sam, Liza, everyone. It was fun to know Liza was lying, to see the lie plainly on her face, like badly applied make-up, and say nothing. "She wants to give me her soul," Ann thought derisively. "What a fake she is. And I'm glad of it. I don't have to feel any conscience about hurting her. She deserves it."

"No, I lied," Liza said, "about the Princess. Tanya wasn't the first. There was one before."

Ann thought, "I bet there were at least ten." But she looked at Liza's longing face and was silent. There was an emotion in the face like a cry for help.

"My singing teacher was the first," said Liza. "Madam Lafollet. I didn't have enough money for lessons. So she took it out in trade."

The inner cry remained in Liza's face as she smiled lewdly at her companion. "Hoping to please me," Ann thought, "as if she were making love to me on different levels. Trying to make me feel pity for her while exciting me with dirty stories at the same time. They're more complex than men."

"I'd like to tell you the truth, Ann, without any whitewash on it."

Ann thought, "Yes, she'd like to. But she can't. She'll lie, so as not to offend me too much. She has to lie even about truths, or she'd frighten herself." A tenderness touched Ann's heart. "Poor little girl," she thought, "getting kicked out by God at eleven."

"Madam Lafollet was a wonderful singing teacher," said Liza. "Very educated and classy. A little old but nice legs. No hips. Flat chested and mean as hell. Talked like an icicle. But, my God. She'd go after me like a mountain lion."

"You liked that?" Ann's glass trembled.

"Oh, yes. It made me feel alive."

"Often?"

"I took two lessons a week."

"Shall we get some more wine?" Ann asked.

"Not for me."

"I'm amazed that you could like both—men and women," Ann said.

"I never liked men, I told you. Please believe me," Liza answered. "I put up with them. I used them. They thought they were using me, of course."

"Use them for what?"

"Money," said Liza. "A good time. And being wanted. It always gave me a kick when they started drooling."

"It used to irritate me," said Ann.

"I thought you didn't know any before Henry or after," Liza smiled.

"I didn't know them," said Ann. "But they drooled just the same. In school, especially. At dances. Parties. Pushing against you and sweating." She shuddered.

"Henry must have had quite a job."

"Seducing me?" Ann smiled. "It was very dull for a time. Until I woke up."

"You really woke up?" Liza looked at her moodily.

"Oh, yes." Ann held out a hand, "Come, fess up. You did, too."

Liza took the hand and put it against her mouth. "No, darling, I didn't."

"Tell me the truth," Ann said.

Liza released her hand. She raised tear-wetted eyes.

"Oh, God, I know how hard it is for anyone to believe me," she said. "I'd rather die than lie to you, Ann. It makes me sick to remember."

"What?"

"The way I faked with him, Henry. The way I never felt anything. The way I carried on."

"That's sad," Ann said. "But I suppose most women are like that."

"It's hard telling," said Liza, "especially for a man. Women lie like bitches. They put on a Ringling Brothers act in bed. With calliope music. I've done it. Whoop and flop around like a sailfish on a pier. Men love it. It gives them a diploma as lovers—when they land a hot one. God, I hate them. Even Henry. Because they're so stupid. Even Henry with all his brains. After he'd seen through me and I admitted the truth—that I couldn't feel, I could only fake and pretend. Even after finding that out, he believed in me again. Two weeks later he believed I was exploding with passion."

"He thought he'd cured you," said Ann.

"That's right," Liza smiled, "and I went along with it."

"Ringling Brothers?"

"Three rings," Liza grinned.

"Poor Henry," Ann smiled.

She stood up and walked to the phone.

"Please tell August to bring up two Martinis," she said to the operator.

"You'll get stewed," Liza said.

"I wouldn't mind," said Ann. "Tell me more about my adored Henry."

"You'll get sad," Liza whispered.

"Sad my foot," said Ann.

"You are sad about him," Liza pouted.

"I tell you I'm not," Ann answered angrily. "I'm amused

—at the thought of what leaping jackasses men are. A man like Henry being taken in by you! Good lord, he should have whipped you with a cat-o'-nine-tails for your faking."

"He did, in a way," said Liza. "That's why I thought I loved him. Because he almost despised me."

"You're too beautiful for anyone to despise thoroughly," Ann smiled suddenly.

"I am?"

"God, yes. Even your feet and ankles."

"Yours are perfect," said Liza. She stood up.

"And when you move," Ann said, "all of you moves. Like an anaconda," she grinned. Liza sat down again on the floor and leaned her head against Ann's knees. Ann took a deep breath.

"Get up," she said.

Liza stood up and went to the window. She stood looking out, her back to Ann's flushed face.

"She knows herself irresistible," Ann thought. "She knows every curve of her rear view."

"It's going to rain," said Liza.

Ann was silent.

"What did I say wrong?" Liza asked, huskily. "Please tell me."

"Your lies about Henry."

"What lies?"

"Your deadness with him."

"I was."

"Oh, don't be childish. You can't fool me. I'm not a man.

You were crazy over Henry. You went wild in bed—probably passed out with ecstasy."

"I didn't. I swear," Liza's throat filled with tears.

"You're a lie, inside and out," Ann said. "If I were a man, I'd whale the truth out of you."

"I've given you the truth," Liza said dully. "I've never given it to anyone else. I've given you every truth I know. Without any cover-up or whitewash."

The doorbell rang. Ann opened it for August, the waiter. She signed for the drinks. August bowed gratefully again. Ann brought a drink to Liza.

"Here, Liza."

Liza turned slowly from the window. Tears were running from her eyes.

"What's the matter?" asked Ann.

"You hate me."

"It isn't hate. It's seeing you. I see you rather clearly."

"Am I that bad?"

"You're not bad. You're just a fake," Ann said. "You act all the time. There isn't an ounce of truth or reality in you."

"I haven't lied to you," Liza said through tears.

"You don't have to lie to be a fake," said Ann. "You're faking now. The way children fake. You're not crying because you feel bad. But to make me feel bad."

"I feel awful."

"You feel nothing," said Ann. "There's nothing in you."

"There is," Liza whispered. "I feel like a swamp."

"No," Ann said, "you want to use me like you used Henry.

Like you'd use anybody. Even a dog, if it suited. To see them drool over you."

"Not you," said Liza.

"Please," Ann smiled. "You've told me the truth. The same truth you told Henry. That you're a freak—a fake without sex. When somebody feels anything for you, you're a big girl. A big hit. A big star in a spotlight—their passion."

"That's always been true before," said Liza, "except once. No, twice. I told you about them."

"I know you did," said Ann. "You told me a lot of things. But now you want me to forget them, as Henry did. And imagine I'm the only one."

"I wish you were," said Liza. "You're the only beautiful one. You're so beautiful. You're perfect. And not mean like the others. The other two. You're just beautiful and perfect." She dried her eyes carefully, sat down and drank.

"Thank you," Ann said, "I'm sorry I sounded off. You sort of drew it out of me."

"I know," said Liza, "people like to criticize me. I mean bright people."

"You're like a jigsaw puzzle," said Ann, "everybody thinks he can put you together correctly. I'm very sorry."

"You shouldn't be," Liza smiled dimly. "I'm a tramp. A nothing. A nothing tramp. Without a heart of gold. I saw a movie once, a western, where the town whore jumped in front of the hero when the villain shot him. She took the bullet. The sheriff leaned over her while she was dying. 'I'm afraid it's the end,' he said. 'He got her right through the heart.' And the dying whore whispered, 'And they always said I didn't have one.'" Liza chuckled. "I'm different."

"Henry told me that episode," Ann sighed. "He learned a lot from you."

"We taught each other," said Liza.

Ann sipped her drink. "She's entertaining," she thought, "a thousand times more than Sam." She thought, suddenly, of the bed in the other room, and her mind grew blank. A confusion filled her body with heat and cold.

"Frankie's the only thing in my life I regret," said Liza, as if there had been no mood or tears before, "the only human being I've ever felt sorry for."

"How can you feel sorry for a cruel man?"

"If you know what makes him cruel," said Liza. "I'm cruel, too. I was cruel to him. I refused to help him."

"You're not a psychiatrist, my dear."

"It was fun refusing. Being cruel."

"Was that why you didn't want him back after the Princess?"

"One reason," said Liza. "The other was it was too much work. It was like breathing into the mouth of a corpse." Ann recognized one of Henry's literary hobbies, Tibetan Yogi stories.

Liza shuddered. "He used to get so happy, he'd cry and blubber over me. Kiss my feet. He called me God."

"That was before the Princess?" Liza nodded. "You didn't want man love after her."

"Yes, in a way. In a kind of warmed-over way, I did," said Liza. Her face grew pale.

"What is it?" Ann asked.

"A wave came over me," said Liza. "Hold my hand, will you?"

Ann took her hand.

"What's the wave like?" she asked.

"It's gone," said Liza. "Something comes into you. Not your head. You don't think anything. But it comes in here." She put a hand under her breast. "A fright. And you know something's coming."

"He isn't coming," said Ann. "He scares you because you hide your mind from him. You're afraid to think of him. So he thinks inside you—by himself."

"You could be right," said Liza. "That white skin of his. Without ankles. Heavy, lumpy legs with thick feet stuck on. And talking about his ma all the time. I mean, when he cried. Which was practically all the time, after the Princess."

"Did you try to resume with him?"

"Yes, I told you."

"You said you couldn't stand him, and had to be cruel."

"I guess that's what you mean by my lies. It's true I couldn't stand him. But it's also true I tried."

"Often?"

"Several times."

"You went to bed?"

"Yes."

"What happened?"

"His craziness would crawl out of him into me. I'd go

crazy, too. I laughed. The more he cried, the more I laughed."

"Were these tries during Sovey's time with you?"

"Yes."

"During Henry's?"

"Once."

"Only once?"

Liza nodded.

"You tried to betray Henry?"

"Yes. I've never admitted that even to myself before. I'd forgotten it."

"What made Frank stop going after you, if he needed and wanted you so much?"

"I wouldn't let him touch me."

"Couldn't he make you? He's so strong."

"That wouldn't help him any. I had to take the lead."

Liza closed her eyes. "I'm getting sleepy," she said.

"It's not late," said Ann.

"I'm going to have a bath," said Liza. "Do you want one first?"

"No, thank you. Go ahead."

Ann thought, "She's acting matter of fact, because she's sure of me. With all that hate of herself and self-disillusion, she still thinks she's irresistible. Whoever she wants must follow her."

Liza stood looking at her.

"Don't hate me," she whispered, and smiled like a child.

"Oh, stop it," Ann said.

"We have no nightgowns."

"I never sleep in them," said Ann.

Liza walked out of the room. Ann sat motionless, the empty glass in her fingers. "I ought to go home," she thought. "I'm not this way. I'm normal. I'm a man's woman. This sort of thing is just depravity. There's no need behind it. Just nerve-ending adventure. It makes me sick." Her head felt pleasantly dizzy.

"She may even be a murderess," she continued. "How can I know anything truthful about her?" She smiled. "It's hard knowing even anything truthful about myself. No, she didn't kill Sovey. Davies did. I'm a fool." A smile filled her. "What a thing to tell Henry. My Liza escapade. Little by little. Lies at first. Evasions. Contradictions. He'll be after me as he was after her. A third degree night after night."

She laughed out loud at the thought of how angry he would be over her final statement—that nothing had actually happened between her and Liza. She stopped the imaginary conversation. Nothing was going to happen. This far it was just fantasy, with a little glandular orchestration. And no real Liza involved. A phantom Liza. The real Liza was crudely different.

"She's a cheap tart," Ann thought. "Raped at eleven. And God knows how many times afterward. I can see her. A little cur dog who answered all the whistles. She's utterly low class. It's amazing that she speaks English correctly. Probably learned in bed from college boys and sugar daddies. And Madam Lafollet. I'll sleep on this couch."

She moved to the sofa, sat down, and took off her shoes.

"No sense in mussing my clothes," she thought. "Thank God there's a door between us."

She walked to it. The brightly lit bedroom was empty. Liza was still bathing. Ann closed the door. She moved cautiously in the darkened room to the couch. "She'll not open that door, I know her. She'll stay put like a stray dog."

Ann stretched out on the couch. It was hard and scratchy. She closed her eyes. "That rotten Henry," she thought. "Men have no character. It's true. Character consists of living with your preferred self. Not setting fire to orphan asylums. Or snatching old ladies' pocketbooks. Or allowing a few little tickles to pull you into a sexual underworld. My preferred self is decency and integrity. I'm decent. I've always been."

She remembered her thousand nights, mornings and mid-days with Henry. The wanton search for sensation. The bestial give and take. She blushed at some of the memories.

"That's different," she thought. "That's all part of marriage." She recalled Henry's words: "Marriage is depravity with a license." So true. No whore could be more depraved than Elsie. Or herself, for that matter. But it was a separate compartment: depravity! What you did in the bathroom, you didn't do in the parlor. What you did in your husband's arms you hid from the world. And from your own memory.

She smiled sleepily at the sounds in the next room. Liza was getting into bed. She hadn't opened the door to pretend to say good night.

"I wonder what she thinks of when she's alone," Ann

213

thought. "All the men who drooled over her. And women. She's really scum. Not even an honest animal with honest glands."

Alcohol glazed her thought and she lay dormant and awake. The faint midnight sounds of the street came through the opened window.

"I must sleep," she thought. "I'm relaxed. My breasts are soft." She touched one with her hand. Her hand remained on her breast. She closed her eyes, but there was no sleep.

The window curtains were flapping. "It's going to storm," she thought. Her hand left her breast. "My God, I haven't even washed my face," she thought, "and I have to use that damn toilet. I'll wait till she's asleep." The wind increased. Thunder sounded in the distance. She looked closely at her wrist watch. It was after one. The minutes passed with an uncomfortable lag. The flapping curtains made a faint, frantic noise. A new odor filled the room with an odd liveliness. It was the rain sending its smell ahead. Lightning flash lighted the windows. A ripping blast of thunder followed, and the rain leaped in the night.

Ann listened to the halloo of falling rain. It wasn't her home. Let it spatter the room.

"No," she thought, "that's silly."

She got up and started for the open window. Then she turned and opened the bedroom door.

The room was dark. Liza lay under a thin sheet. Her black hair made a violent scrawl on the white pillow. The head was motionless, its eyes closed.

Ann stood beside the bed. The smell and the noise of the

rain brought long-ago memories into the darkened room. She remembered a little girl staring at her sleeping mother.

"Did the storm wake you up?" Ann whispered.

There was no answer from the pillow. Ann lay down in the bed, a foot away from the naked body.

"I haven't awakened her," she thought, and remained motionless.

Liza's head turned slowly toward her.

❧

Dark morning was in the windows. Ann looked at the ebbing storm. The rain fell thinly.

Liza was asleep beside her. The white teeth glistened between their heavy lips.

"Liza," she said. The girl remained in a deep sleep. An exhaustion was in her breathing. Ann shook Liza's shoulder. The face remained inert, the deep breathing continued.

Ann sat up. She pulled the sheet down. Liza lay there sleeping. Ann closed her eyes slowly, and pulled the sheet back and stepped out of bed. She looked around for her slip.

It was on the floor at the head of the bed. Ann picked it up and went into the bathroom. She came out in a half hour.

"I'll leave her a note," she walked into the other room and wrote on hotel stationery: "Have gone to raise our troops. Will phone you around noon. Ann."

She added, "P.S. Please don't go away."

Returning to the bedroom, she pinned the note on her

215

pillow. Liza still slept as if only trumpets could waken her.

"Good-by," she said softly to the heavily sleeping face. "I hope you wake up happy."

She rode downstairs. In the lobby she saw a familiar figure. It was the short, fat man who looked like an underworld comedian, the one who had ogled her and Liza while they registered. He was evidently done with ogling for he avoided her eyes.

"Queer types in a hotel like this," she thought, and then smiled at the gloomy, rain-washed street. What type could be queerer than her own?

In the taxi heading for Henry's office, she thought, "He may guess the whole thing the moment he sees me. My eyes feel like cinders. And he knows I've been with her. Well, if he guesses, what's it matter?" She shivered. "It's odd that I don't feel any conscience pangs," she thought. "It's really amazing."

Ann looked into her compact mirror.

"Nothing's changed," she thought. "I must remember that I'm exactly as I am, minus a few invisible pretenses. And my eyes a bit hollowed out."

The taxi holed up in a traffic jam. Ann lit a cigarette. "There's no hurry," she thought, and closed her eyes so she could daydream.

Henry sat at the restaurant table with Sam and Vangie—number three in his confession. He sipped his coffee and

glanced at his watch. The Police Commissioner had said ten
o'clock. They could leave in thirty minutes and arrive on
time.

Sam talked to Vangie. Listening to him, Henry thought,
"The whinnying husband. A revolting type."

"It's a perfect job for a girl like you," said Sam, "not just
secretarial. What I want is a campaign co-ordinator. Someone to be at my side in all the political running around.
Publicity and speeches and that sort of thing."

"It sounds divine," said Vangie.

Henry thought, "The sex maneuvers of another male are
always repulsive." He looked at Vangie and winced at his
own lack of taste. A tall, blondined, stupid girl who seemed
like a line of accessories on sale. A detachable mouth—guar-
anteed to kiss like a nymph and talk like a nitwit. An Italian
hairdo, ardor resistant. Globular front, like a pair of green
traffic lights. The rest of the stock was invisible under the
table.

"I must have been interested in her character," Henry
thought, "of which there is none. I mustn't overdo my new
virtue. Availability was the only thing in a woman that attracted me."

He finished his coffee.

"You feel sure the Commissioner will take the sergeant
off the case?" he asked.

"What? Oh, yes," Sam said. "No question of it." He looked
archly at Vangie, "We're very good friends, the Commissioner and I. You'll get to meet him. Interesting fellow."

"How wonderful," said Vangie.

"I'll go upstairs and have a look at the mail," said Henry. He stood up. Vangie also stood up.

"I'll go with you," she said. "I have a number of things to finish up."

Sam looked unhappy. "I'll wait here, Henry."

"Be right down," said Henry.

"What time shall I be at your office, Mr. Hartnett?" Vangie asked.

"About noon will be all right," said Sam. "I may be a few minutes late. But I'd like to get started soon as possible." He added pompously to Henry, "I've got three speeches to dictate. My opening Englewood gems."

"Can't wait to hear them," said Henry.

Vangie was moody in the elevator. So was Henry.

"I imagine I was hoping to reform her," he thought at her side. "The usual husband complex. They like to make a wife half whore and turn a whore into a wife."

He walked through his anteroom into his well-furnished office. Vangie followed him.

Henry sat at his desk and started opening mail.

"Can I speak to you, just a minute?" Vangie asked.

"Go ahead."

"Do you really want me to go work for Mr. Hartnett?"

"Yes. It's a very good job."

"I know but—oh, Henry, I love you so.'

"Thanks."

"It's been so wonderful."

Henry nodded.

218

"It'll only be for a couple of months, won't it?" asked Vangie.

"That's up to you."

"I'll not let him touch me, Henry. I swear by my father and mother. I'll be true to you every minute."

"It isn't necessary," said Henry.

"I wish you hadn't said that," said Vangie. "It shows what you think of me."

"You're all right," Henry said, reading a letter from an outraged novelist. No ads in any literary section for three weeks. He put the letter in his pocket and stood up. "You're a fine girl." He would have to walk by her now and avoid a final embrace and possible finale on the couch.

"My wife should be here soon," he said. "Tell her I'm at the Commissioner's office with Sam and that I'll be back around eleven. And that I'll call her here and give her the news in case I'm delayed."

"Yes," said Vangie.

"And you be at Sam's office at noon," he said briskly. "I'll probably see you in Englewood, during the campaign."

He was in safe territory, near the door. "You look great, Vangie. Really beautiful in that getup. I'll miss you."

"No, you won't."

"Let's not argue," Henry smiled and opened the door.

"Oh, I feel so sad," Vangie sighed. "Aren't you even going to kiss me good-by?"

"No," said Henry, "a kiss is hello, never good-by. Be a good girl."

He was out of the door and felt exultant as if all his sins

had been washed away. Hurrying to the elevator, he thought of Ann, "I've never loved her before. No, not like this. With an undivided me."

Vangie looked at herself in the wall mirror and listened to her twenty-second lover make good his escape. The number twenty-two made her frown. It seemed too high. She pondered. "But I said twenty-two when it started. Oh, I see." She smiled. She remembered something and changed the number to nineteen, and felt much better.

She was at her desk in the reception room when Ann appeared. Mrs. Lawrence always made her feel guilty and very nervous. But there was nothing to feel guilty about any more.

"Good morning, Vangie," Ann smiled.

"Good morning, Mrs. Lawrence."

"Is Mr. Lawrence in?"

"Not yet," said Vangie. "He's at the Police Commissioner's office with Mr. Hartnett. He'll be back any minute, I'm sure."

Vangie opened the publisher's sanctum. Ann entered it.

"High and mighty," Vangie thought. "I'd like to tell her a thing or two. Would she start screaming!" Vangie smiled sweetly at the visitor.

"Thank you, Vangie," said Ann.

She looked at the girl smirking at her in the doorway and thought, "What a gangling trollop. She must have bored Henry to death. She's as sexless as a barber pole."

"I thought I'd tell you, Mrs. Lawrence, that I'm leaving here and going to work for Mr. Hartnett," said Vangie.

"Oh, really," Ann offered her suburbia smile, "that should be very interesting."

"I've always been fascinated by politics," Vangie said.

"Yes. Much more exciting than literature," Ann said, vaguely. She thought of Sam waiting eagerly for this oafish blonde. What a farce it was, wives, husbands and catch-as-catch-can sweeties.

"Good luck, Vangie," she smiled.

"Thank you," Vangie watched the publisher's wife sit down on the couch. "Our couch," she thought, and said good-by to it more tenderly than she had to Henry. She wondered what kind of a wife Mr. Hartnett had. And what kind of a couch.

Ann waited till the door closed and stretched out on Vangie's lost domain.

"Henry's arena," she thought, "obviously his jousting field —the way she looked at me sitting in it. Poor girl, they haven't many rights." She frowned and tried to think angrily. But her sense of joy was too strong. Henry and his trollops were far away, even on this couch. They were unable to intrude on her daydream.

She lay, eyes closed, and remembered, and planned.

Morning wakened Sergeant Davies in Greta Gretz's shabby room. He sat up quickly. His mouth was sticky dry. He looked around for water. He saw the blue bathrobe beside him and frowned. He looked into the dead face and saw the bulging throat. His skin chilled.

He started dressing, his eyes on the dead girl. He was unable to swallow, as if something were sticking in his throat. A thought came. He repeated it as he dressed—"I'll go to the Captain and give myself up." He knew he wouldn't, but it was pleasant to want to. But not for too long. "It's better the other way," he thought. He didn't have to think of what the other way was. It was the other Frank Davies, the one who lived in a red mist.

He left the rooming house without seeing anyone. He thought, "I got to move fast, before they find Greta."

Half an hour later, he stood in the hallway looking at Liza King's apartment door. He opened it with a key and stood looking at its furnishings. The chill left his skin. Blood filled his neck. An eagerness smiled from his face. He walked out into the hall, closed Liza's door. He opened the apartment door across the hall.

Tin Can lay on the couch, naked and sleeping. He shook her. She opened reddened eyes.

"Get me a fix," he said.

"I was havin' a dream," the girl said. She sat up. "What time is it? Oh, I'm goin' to die."

"Get moving. I want a boost."

"Give a girl time," she scowled. "Come into bed with me. I'm cold. My belly's frozen. Feel me. I'm ice cold."

The sergeant whacked the side of her head with his thick hand. Her scream pleased him. "You want more?"

"No," the girl said. She found her kimono and went to

the closet at the other end of the room. She came back with two hypodermics.

"Same as last night," Davies said.

"Sure."

He uncovered his arm.

"You want some breakfast?" the girl asked.

"No," he went to the phone and dialed. "Hello, Sergeant Davies," he said into the phone. "MacFarland around?" The voice answered, "Not yet, Frank. You goin' to bed or wakin' up?"

"Wakin' up," Davies said.

"We got a call here you might check on Liza King, if you think it's worth while. A fella called in from some hotel."

"Let's have it," said Sergeant Davies. He stood listening as the room around him grew warm and bright.

Sergeant Frank Davies stopped his prowl car in front of the Montgomery Hotel. He picked up a package from its seat, put it under his raincoat and left the car.

He stood motionless in the hotel lobby. After several moments, the short, fat man with the comedian's face came to him.

"Lookin' for somebody?" the man asked.

"I'm Detective Sergeant Frank Davies," he answered.

"I thought so," the fat one said. "I'm the house detective who phoned in the information. Kid McGuire. She's up in thirty-three."

"Still there?"

"Yeh. The redhead left. But the one ya want's on ice. Funny. I had a hunch when she come in to register last night. And when I seen her pictures in the papers afterward I called ya right away. I left word for ya to be notified."

"Thanks."

"Here's the key," said Kid McGuire. "My passkey. Can I do anything else for ya, Sarge?"

"No, thanks. I'll be up there quite a while. Examining her. I don't want any interruptions."

"I'll take care of that," said Kid McGuire.

Sergeant Davies walked into an elevator cage. He kept his eyes half closed. He didn't want anyone to look into them.

The door opened noiselessly and the blond sergeant stepped into the room. His eyes opened. He grinned and walked into the bedroom.

"Ah," he said softly, "you're asleep. Liza's asleep." He chuckled and repeated childishly, "She's asleep. Sleep. Sleep. She's asleep."

He stood waiting for several minutes, soundless and motionless. Suddenly he lifted his foot and kicked the body under the sheet with his heel.

Liza groaned and opened her eyes. The sleep daze was still in them.

"Hello," said Davies. "Lie still."

He sat down on the bed and pulled the sheet off her. She stared at him. Suddenly she saw his eyes and started to scream. His thick hand crushed her mouth. She tried wildly

224

to free herself. The sergeant took his club from his pocket. He hit her temple. A bone broke and blood flowed.

Liza lay still. He removed his hand from her mouth, and took the package from under his coat. It contained several medical instruments, a washcloth and a coil of thin rope.

"In case you come to," he said. "I don't want you making any noise, Liza. And spoiling my fun."

His voice was low and mocking. He stuffed the washcloth into the half-open mouth, and stepped quickly into the bathroom. He returned with two damp towels. He covered the mouth with these and then tied them in place with the thin rope. He cut the rope with one of the razor-sharp instruments. Another length of rope tied her wrists behind her. The legs came next. He tied an ankle to each side of the bed.

"Now the neck, Liza," he said. "Liza's nice long neck."

He tied a noose around it. The noose had two long ends. He fastened each of them to the siding of the bed.

Blood continued to seep from Liza's temple. Her eyes opened. Their blueness became alive. She moved weakly under the binding ropes.

"You're awake," Davies said. His voice was happy. "That's very good. That's a help, Mama. Because Frankie wants you to know what he's going to do. Mama, Mama, you're so beautiful. Makes me almost cry. That soft belly. Don't wiggle, please. Your wiggling days are over. Now listen, Mama, I want you to know what Frankie's going to do." He began whispering excitedly. "So you can appreciate what's coming in case you pass out too soon. Or die too soon. Don't die too soon. Stay alive and watch Frankie. He's going to take something out of you. All the little things that make you tick. That make you tick, Mama. But first, we'll try this. It's a friend. See it?"

He held up his policeman's club. He bent over the naked body, chuckling and grunting as he worked. Agony burned in Liza's eyes. A blood vessel broke in one of them and the blue pupil turned red.

The sergeant straightened, his deed done.

"Now we'll start operating," he said. "Take out everything. Frankie wants to see Mama's insides. And take them apart. Frankie's going to send everybody a separate piece for Christmas. Including the Princess. She gets a kidney with a yellow ribbon on it. But they'll all get a piece. You understand. Do you hear Frankie?"

Sergeant Davies picked up one of the thin surgical knives.

"Frankie will begin here," he said. He held the knife motionless in front of Liza's face. "Look, look," he said slowly, "look what's going into you. Now!"

He leaned over and cut a deep gash through the lower abdomen. Blood gushed into the bed. It squirted over his arms and into his face. Pausing only to change his knife for a surgical scissors, Sergeant Davies continued to cut, dig and snip. He hummed and chuckled as Liza's blood turned him redder and redder.

After an hour, the sergeant stopped. His fingers were tired. His hands were numb. A red crust covered his face. He could see only a red mist. The ring of the doorbell turned his head slowly.

"Come in," he called. But no sound came from him. He tried to call again but his voice had disappeared.

The door opened. Sergeant Davies removed his service revolver from its holster. He placed the barrel in his mouth and pulled the trigger. There was a loud bang, and his skull top hopped into the air.

Five people stood in the doorway. Ann saw only a red bed and a dismembered leg on the floor before she fainted. The others saw more. Detective MacFarland knelt beside the blood-soaked Davies.

"He's not dead yet," he said.

Davies' eyes were open.

"Hello, Mac," he said. "I closed the case."

The sergeant's half head rolled to the side. MacFarland stood up.

"Call the precinct," he said to a uniformed policeman. "Go ahead. Call 'em for me."

He leaned against the wall.

The black-robed nun came noiselessly into the small bare-walled convent room. She stood motionless, her young life-drained face looking at Ann Lawrence in the narrow bed. Ann's head was turned away on the pillow and the nun breathed deeply. Her pale eyes glowed. She covered her face suddenly with her hands and lowered her head, as if drawing a curtain over her senses.

"I'm not sleeping," Ann whispered, "please stay, Margo."

"Not Margo," the nun was erect and smooth voiced. "Sister Angela."

"I keep forgetting," said Ann. Her eyes stared at the black robe as at a closed door. She looked up at the almost too youthful face. "Because you haven't changed," she said.

"Yes, I have," said the nun.

"I mean your face," Ann said.

"You are feeling better?" the sister asked.

"Yes," Ann said, "no more nightmares. I slept for an hour and nothing happened. It's gone. You've sent it away. I'm quite ashamed of myself for carrying on the way I have."

"Your mind was torn," said the nun. "A memory can leave a tear in the mind."

Ann closed her eyes and waited for the memory to come dreadfully into the darkness. But nothing came. The name Liza remained unillustrated in her head. She searched cautiously for the unbearable picture. It was nowhere. "She's gone," Ann thought. "Margo has cured me." Something else was also gone—not the butchershop thing on the red bed but Liza herself. There was no more than a name in her mind, that might be anybody's name.

"Can you stay a while, Sister?"

"It's late," the nun said.

"We used to start talking at midnight. Remember?"

"Yes, I remember," the nun said, and sat down in a wooden chair near the bed. "Sister Martha is pleased with your progress. She's certain that there's a place for you as a teacher here. If you still want it."

228

"I don't want it."

"You said you did, Ann."

"Because I was afraid you'd send me home. What I want is to be like you." She looked eagerly at Margo—Sister Angela. "Instead of being eleven years older you're eleven years younger."

"You are interested in our beauty treatment," the nun smiled. "You can get better permanents in New York."

"That's a mean remark," Ann said. "I'm surprised a nun would make it."

"I'm talking to an old friend," said Sister Angela, "with an old set of words."

"Is it all right for you to sit here and talk, Margo? I mean, Sister."

"Yes," the nun said, "you are my charge. I'm responsible for your not disturbing the Sacred Heart Convent with nocturnal shrieks."

"You always had a sharp tongue," Ann said, "and I love it. I'm glad you still have it. Do you still write poetry?"

"Yes," the nun said.

Ann looked at the hooded pale face that seemed part of the moonlight in the room. It was the face of her college dormitory nights, but the familiarity was out of it. "Like a faded photograph," she thought. And Margo's voice was also different. It spoke to no one.

"I've thought of you very often," the nun said. "That's why I wrote to you when I read you were ill in the hospital."

"You saved my life," Ann said, "or at least you got me out of bed. I thought I'd stay there forever. And now—" she

229

raised her arms in the air as if embracing the moonlit room. Her linen nightgown opened and her flesh shone. "It's wonderful how things can go away," she said softly. "Everything. Sin, horror, pain . . . they all go, don't they?"

"Yes," said the nun, "they can be discarded."

"That's what I want to do," Ann said, "discard everything."

She looked at the nun's hands. They rested in the black lap like strangers—to the nun. They were Margo's hands, unchanged—the hands that had helped her dry her hair, that had sewed on party dresses and held books of poetry and psychiatry. They were still soft fingered and unfaded. They moved as if Sister Angela were about to arise and go.

"Talk to me about God," Ann said.

"You're bribing me," the nun said.

"That's your meanness again," Ann said.

"The way you used to bribe me by asking me to read Sigmund Freud when you couldn't sleep, and when I loved Freud." Sister Angela remained in the chair.

"You don't love him any more?"

"I still read him sometimes," said the nun. "He's nice, like Mother Goose."

"About God?" Ann said, softly. She turned on her side and looked at the young mysterious face of her friend. "Maybe it's only the hood that makes it mysterious," she thought.

"Do you remember," the nun said, "when I used to look out of our window at college and remark on how well run the universe was? All those planets and galaxies and nebulae leaping about in some incomprehensible ballet. That's God."

"But you didn't pray to that ballet," said Ann.

"I don't pray to it now," said the nun. "Nobody prays to God. That would be presumptuous."

"Really? To whom do you pray, then?"

"I pray the way a good servant cleans house," said the nun. "Prayer is my daily house cleaning. It removes the dust of the world from your spirit. It enables you to participate."

"In the ballet," said Ann.

"In God."

"Isn't that odd theology?" Ann asked, and thought, "She's not changed. She's bright and alive. The same fun to talk to. The same wonderful fun."

"I'm not a theologian," the nun smiled. "Theology offers proofs of God. When Bishop Carroway was here, I told him I didn't wish to waste my time reading about proofs of God in long, deplorable sentences."

"But the Bishop doesn't write like that," said Ann, eagerly, "he has a magnificent style."

"Bishop Carroway is proof of the fact that a writer can love God without ruining his vocabulary," said the nun.

Ann looked intently at the pretty face of her once dearest friend, the only intimate face of her youth after her mother had been killed. The quietude of the face was soothing. But it was still a face that fascinated. It had always had secrets—a thin nose, pale eyes and high cheekbones full of secrets. Now its secrets seemed more important. Ann sighed.

231

She wanted her own face to be like Margo's. She wanted the glow of Margo's spirit to fill her own being—to be able to think of nothing more personal than the universe and the pleasant antlike chores of the convent. She reached out from the bed and took Margo's hand. Its warmth surprised her, as if it were a denial of the pale, emotionless face and its aloof, colorless eyes.

"Sister Angela," said Ann, "will you help me? I don't want to go back in the world."

"We'll talk of it later," Margo's hand remained in hers, warm and beating.

"I don't want to go back to my husband, or to anybody," Ann said. "I have hardly any memory of them. Or of anything. I want to belong to your universe. And clean house like you."

"I understand," the nun's hand squeezed the fingers around it. Ann's mind became blank. The warm pressure on her fingers brought a lightness to her. Closing her eyes, she whispered, "Help me, Margo."

Sister Angela answered, "I will, Ann."

Bishop Carroway sat in his stone-walled study adjoining the cathedral and listened to the nun from the Sacred Heart Convent in New Jersey.

"Her name is Ann Lawrence," said Sister Angela. "She has been in retreat in our convent for two weeks and wishes to become a nun."

"I remember reading about her," said the Bishop. "Murders, and all that. She wants to become a nun, eh? Too bad."

"I think she should be dissuaded," said Sister Angela.

"Have you tried dissuading her?" the Bishop asked.

"No," Sister Angela said.

"Why haven't you?"

"Poetry has other uses," the nun smiled.

"I don't like cryptic statements," said Bishop Carroway, "particularly smug ones."

The nun nodded. The Bishop was her favorite man of God. He was a plump, wise and annoying scholar, able to recite whole books of poetry from memory. And he despised bad conversation as much as he did the Devil. Most of the sisters considered him a disturbing influence and avoided, as much as they could, speaking to him. Sister Martha said of the Bishop: "That holy man can undermine the faith of a saint. I'm sure he secretly thinks that all people who believe in God are idiots." Sister Angela answered her: "Perhaps he thinks that believing in God doesn't make a person less an idiot."

She looked now at the mass of books along the stone walls, at the tapestries on the high walls, and the circular stone staircase at the rear of the study—and felt as if she were on a stage with a heroic character.

"I'm sorry to seem smug," she said. "I hope I usually don't. But you bring it out in me—as a defense. Because you have a better mind than I have."

"I have that," said the Bishop.

233

"You also have the advantage over me of having heard my confessions," said Sister Angela. "I have never heard yours."

"I'll give them to you in a nutshell," the Bishop said. "I'm a worse sinner than you are. But a much brighter one. Now take that melancholy look off your face and I'll forgive you for talking like a fortuneteller. Honest words, Sister. What is this whole thing about and why do you bother me with it?"

"Ann is an old friend of mine," said the nun, "and always liked to imitate me—in a superficial way."

"Naturally," the Bishop sneered, "you being inimitable."

Sister Angela smiled. "Do you want to hear what I have to say on the subject?"

"Not remotely," said the Bishop, "but there's no stopping you. Go on."

"I know what would happen if I tried arguing with Ann," she said. "It would just increase her insistence and make her emotional. She was always able to mistake her hysteria for sincerity."

"An easy error," said the Bishop.

"She has read your books," Sister Angela said, "and admires them very much. Even the parts she couldn't understand."

"An imbecile, eh?" said the Bishop.

"Comparatively."

"Is she pretty?" asked the Bishop.

"Very."

"How old?"

"My age," said Sister Angela.

"And well-to-do, I presume," said the Bishop.

"Her husband is a successful man."

"Who preferred another," the Bishop sneered, "and so she loves him no longer."

"It's more complicated than that," said Sister Angela.

"It always is," the Bishop sighed. He looked at the ceiling and asked, "Have you ever referred to this aspirant for holiness in the past, Sister Angela?"

"She is the only one I've ever referred to," the nun answered. A redness was in her cheeks. Bishop Carroway continued to look at the ceiling.

"Tell her to come in," he said, "and you wait outside. She will rejoin you shortly." His eyes looked at the hooded face in front of him. "And don't worry, Sister," he said, "she will not bring pain to your convent."

Ann entered the study alone. She saw a gray-haired man in a priest's habit, but with an unpriestly face. It was plump and red cheeked like a Franz Hals portrait, but it offered no look of sanctity. It had round, clownlike eyes, inky and exuberant eyebrows, a smile-curved mouth and a general air of deviltry. The Bishop neither arose nor spoke as she entered.

Ann said, "I am very grateful to you, Father, for the favor. I know how busy you are. Allow me to thank you, Father, for taking the time to see me."

"I shall feel that the time is not wasted, Mrs. Lawrence," the Bishop answered, "if you use your natural voice. I get very depressed when people speak to me as if they were clinging to an altar rail."

"I'm sorry if I seem so artificial, Father."

"You do," said Bishop Carroway, "please speak to me and not to my black robe. I am the one who is listening."

"You remind me of—" Ann stopped at the name Henry.

"I usually remind people of someone they don't like," the Bishop said. "Tell me about your husband."

"He's dead," said Ann, coolly, "that is, he's dead in my mind. But quite alive elsewhere."

"Have you spoken to him since the tragic death of his inamorata?" the Bishop asked.

"No," said Ann. "I was in the hospital for two days and went from there to Margo's convent. I mean Sister Angela. I've had no urge to speak to my husband. I have no anger or argument in me. Or even memory of him. I spent the two weeks in the convent preparing myself."

"For your new life," said the Bishop.

"Yes," said Ann. "I want to become a novitiate and to take holy Orders."

"And turn your back on the world," the Bishop said, "and be done with its many fevers."

"I want to serve only God," said Ann, and kept her eyes on her unfriendly sounding interlocutor.

"Whom have you been serving till now?" he asked.

"Myself," said Ann, "and no one."

"Sister Teresa's answer in 1409 before the inquisitors of Seville," said the Bishop. "Please give me one of your own."

Ann was silent, but decided not to cry.

"Take your time," he said, "the desire for sanctity is often inarticulate."

"I don't want to live in the world," Ann said suddenly. "I want to leave the world. I want to be out of it, entirely."

"The world is yourself, Mrs. Lawrence."

"I know," she said.

"It is unmedical as well as impractical to try to live away from oneself," the Bishop said.

"I can worship God and live in Him," Ann's voice pleaded.

"I have seen many women kneeling in church trying to worship God," said the Bishop. "It is a very difficult thing to do. It takes an important Holy Day to bring Him into their hearts, even for a brief service. As a lifetime job," the Bishop grinned suddenly, "worshiping God can be a tremendous bore."

"You wrote that in your last book," said Ann. "It startled me. And convinced me that I was one of those God would never bore."

"A brash statement," the Bishop said, "considering your capacity for boredom. The world has bored you. And so has your husband."

"I'm sure God is different," Ann smiled.

"He may well be," said the Bishop, "but you are the same. I am not a great authority on the female. But I have noted one facet of their natures—their manner of worshiping God. It usually arises out of an anger toward the men with whom they are bedded. Or sometimes it is a substitute for men missing from their beds. And most often, of course, God is just something to do—like shopping, or a superior club meeting."

"I would like to explain about myself," Ann said.

"Please don't," the Bishop beamed suddenly. "Just sit quietly for a while until I get used to your beauty of face and body—and can study your problem without abstraction."

Ann leaned back in her carved wooden chair and tried to recite an orison in her mind. But the Bishop's attitude was too stimulating for prayer. She felt rather a call to argument. She remained obediently quiet, however, and examined her feelings about Henry. She was certain the inquiry would center around her wifely duties. But she had told Margo the truth about Henry. He had no more existence in her mind than a story read and forgotten.

After a minute of silence, she said, "My desire to become a nun has nothing to do with any wish to revenge myself on my husband. Nor do I think that dedicating myself to God will repair my social standing. The whole truth is, I've found peace and the only happiness I've ever known working with the Sisters of the Sacred Heart."

"For two weeks," the Bishop said.

"For as long as I live," said Ann.

"I dislike arguments about tomorrow," Bishop Carroway said. "Today is sufficiently hidden. You have had a great sorrow and have been able, with the aid of ritual and discipline, to turn your back on it."

"Is that wrong, Father?"

"Yes," he said, "it is wrong to turn your back on anything, sorrow included. Have you thought of consulting a psychiatrist?"

"I thought the Church didn't approve of them," Ann said.

"The science of psychiatry," said the Bishop, "is a minor rival. It is much too expensive ever to be a menace to religion. Whether I approve or not, I have noticed that it can comfort wealthy women afflicted with sexual problems that cannot be mended by sermons."

"I have no sexual problems," said Ann. "I want to live only with my spirit." Margo had been moved by this statement a week ago. The Bishop wasn't.

"Oho," he said, and his clownlike eyes brightened as if light had entered his mind, "we are tired of the sins of the body."

"Yes," said Ann.

"Have there been many? I ask only because you impress me as a virtuous woman."

"I was once," said Ann.

"Aren't you now?"

"I have been to confession and been absolved," Ann said, "and I am again. Virtuous. Decidedly."

"Good," the Bishop said, "then your problem is solved. And there is no need to shave your head."

"You're making fun of me," said Ann. He offered no contradiction. Ann shivered. "He sees through me," she thought, and felt confused. There was nothing to see through. Unless Margo had told him something. But there was nothing for Margo to have told. She had wept in Margo's arms for two nights. But that had been from shock. Margo—Sister Angela had healed her more than the doctor and nurses with their injections.

"I am a sort of amateur psychiatrist," said the Bishop. "I have read many of their books. And I have also a couch of my own, so to speak, from which to study so-called neurotics. The confessional. So I shall ask a rather professional question. Did your loss of virtue involve a woman rather than a man?"

Ann stared and was silent.

"I see," said the Bishop, "your silence says a woman. I imagined as much when you started speaking. You have that firm voice, bright mind and strong hands I have noted in other females who feel themselves misnamed. Sappho often sends for God as a physician. But He is not a specialist." He smiled at Ann. "I understand now why your husband seems undesirable enough to you to be called dead. I understand."

"I'm not like that," Ann said, and stopped.

"Go on," the Bishop looked at the ceiling.

"I'm afraid," Ann said.

"That means that your intelligence is returning," said the Bishop. "You came in here like a sleepwalker."

Ann remained silent. Memories came to her. She tried to keep Margo's face in her mind. But it drifted off. In its place came Liza's face. Not the wrecked face on the red bed, but a Liza unimpaired. Like a radiant actress taking a curtain bow after a brutal death scene. The Liza face grew in her mind and a longing for it returned to her. As if the Liza of the blue eyes and devoted lips were waiting for her somewhere. The longing became a desire to cry out. And suddenly, for the first time since that abhorrent thing on the red bed, a memory flowed through her as if a new blood stream had been released—"Liza, I love you. Darling. Only you."

Ann stared at the Bishop as he started talking, "Dear madam, sexual oddity such as you fancy yourself to have is no excuse for cutting yourself off from the world. There is hardly a human being—and I'm speaking of the good, pious humans who come to church—who isn't the victim of some sexual perversity. There are women who sinfully love animals, chauffeurs—often colored ones—inanimate objects, drunken strangers, close relatives, and, of course, each other. And God knows what else. We live in a disordered time and the sex glands of our world are apparently as confused as its statesmen. Not to mention its clergy. Imagine what trouble we are in for, I mean theological trouble, if we arrive on the planet Venus and discover that its inhabitants were not graced by a visit from our Saviour. As for our own little area of existence and its little sexual confusions, I have always disapproved of converting a deviated libido into a worship of God. In fact, I think it even dangerous. Most of the religious failings in the world's history are due to sex perversion trying to heal itself with prayers and flagellations of various sorts. Usually wars, schisms and unreadable books are the result. The Church has a much safer place for sinners—in its congregation. You can pray there on Sundays, Mrs. Lawrence."

"How do you know about me?" Ann asked, and closed

her eyes. She wanted to fall to her knees in front of the black robe and cry out the name Liza as if it were the name of heaven.

"Disturbances such as yours set up an echo in me," said the Bishop. "Please look at me and stop wallowing in your sins. Perhaps I can help you. It is difficult to remove sin, but sometimes easy to give it a proper proportion. People make a great to-do about sexual activity—as if it were a science or an art. Or worse, a religious failing. I imagine it can be a nuisance, particularly if it gets a bit antisocial or, as they say, perverse. But so can the functioning of our other animal organs. But a malfunctioning kidney or an off-liver do not require repentance. Our human honesty and our relation to God are equally independent of our sexual apparatuses. We do not pick them out. They come in a sealed package. You are not a sinner, madam, but a minor invalid, with a fine character for a doctor." He beamed intently and held out his hand. Ann took it. "Perhaps I shall see you again," the Bishop said, "if your spiritual ambitions persist. I assure you they can wait. The love of God that brings people to His exclusive service is not a quality that can be watered down by time. Come back to me in one year and say to me only that you wish to become a nun and I shall use what influence I have to help you to your goal."

Ann, standing, smiled at Bishop Carroway. Her mind was calm and aware.

"You talk more like a man than a priest," she said, "and although I dislike men, I shall take your advice."

"Bless you," said the Bishop with a boyish grin.

242

Ann preceded him to the door of his study. Sister Angela was waiting in the small vestibule room.

"I took the liberty of calling up your husband at his office," said Sister Angela. "He's waiting outside in his car."

"You asked the Bishop to discourage me," Ann said. Sister Angela nodded. "You lied to me," Ann continued, "you said you would help me."

"I have," the nun said.

Ann looked at her boldly, at the pretty and faded face and the all-hiding nun's habit. "You didn't want me with you, did you?" she asked.

"No," said the nun.

"Because you're more truthful than I am," said Ann.

"I once loved you," Sister Angela said, "and I have had eleven years to understand myself—with the help of God and poetry."

"How sweet you are," Ann said, and held out her hand.

Sister Angela smiled and ignored the gesture. "Your husband is a fine-looking man," she said. "Write me a letter sometime. Good-by, Ann. My dear."

Sister Angela turned and walked quickly toward the door of the Bishop's study.

❧

Henry lay on top of the bed, in dark pajamas, fur slippers and a claret-colored robe. It was a more formal attire than he usually offered in a bedroom. But formality was the new quality in his eight-year-old marriage. He and Ann enjoying, as their friends believed, a second honeymoon had occupied nightly twin beds in the Marguery Hotel of Bermuda without once straying from their separate roosts. He might as well, thought Henry morosely, be honeymooning with Sam Hartnett—at least they could have played backgammon after dark.

The tropic night overwhelmed the opened hotel room windows with what struck him as an uninteresting magnificence. Henry smoked a cigar and turned his eyes from the avalanche of stars to the bathroom door. "I ought to go in there and carry her out à la Sabine," he thought, "but her formality is catching. Besides, raping one's own wife could be ludicrous." The jest of it was that he had never loved her before in this fashion, with heart and truth and a curious humility.

Ann came out of the bathroom. She was in her Chinese robe with nightgown and bed jacket under it. Chinese slippers were on her feet.

"Still heavily armored," thought Henry. He remained silent and tried to look as handsome as he could.

"I've got a good sunburn," Ann said, "both arms and midriff. Tomorrow I'll work on my back."

"I'm resisting a joke," said Henry.

"Yes, I know." She quoted, " 'a woman's place is on her back.' "

"Duffy used to say that while we were still battling the feminist blitz," Henry said. Duffy was the retired partner of his publishing firm.

"Duffy is a despicable man," said Ann.

"Aren't we all?" Henry sighed. "Mind if I keep on smoking my cigar?"

"No, Henry. It's reassuring."

"You promised to tell me more about the Bishop."

"I've told you everything," Ann answered. "We only spoke for thirty minutes."

"The Bishop is an ass," said Henry. "He should have welcomed you to the fold. You'd have made a fascinating nun."

"I don't like to joke about it. Do you mind?"

"I have no desire to joke about your Bishop," Henry said. "I feel too grateful to him. I was just hoping he was a topic that might interest you."

Ann's eyes noted some newspapers and magazines on the floor. Henry thought, "She's going to tidy up, damn it." He remembered ruefully that even on their original honeymoon she had been as neat as an Oriental. But the second "honeymoon," launched after much debate, seemed to have hit a cul-de-sac of neatness and chastity. He watched her lithe movements. Her eyes, voice and gestures were abstract, as if her senses were elsewhere. He thought, "I hurt her too much. All I can do is wait until she asks me to take the hurt away. I mustn't frighten her into deeper frigidity. But I must make her believe in me. That I'm honest."

Waiting, he loved her as if he had never yet touched her. Ann stood reading one of the papers she had picked up.

"The news is pretty bad," she said.

"News is always bad," Henry said, "that's why it's news."

"This is worse," she said.

"I don't care about news," Henry smiled. "I have no interest in major events, except one named Ann."

"Thank you," said Ann, "this seems to be a rather serious war scare."

"Yes, it's become a sort of permanent scare," Henry sighed, "and it's taken the place of nearly everything else."

Ann thought, "Thank heaven, I've got him thinking about something else than my body."

"The threat of atomic war and our subsequent global suicide is our new religion," said Henry. "It's taken the place of our forefathers' concern with original sin, eternal damnation, etcetera. Religion is always a hobby for the old. And this one is an ideal religion for elderly statesmen and editorial writers. Old men are secretly thrilled, I'm sure, at the possibility of the whole world dying with them."

He stopped talking and thought, "She's trying to keep this damn honeymoon on a war basis."

"But everybody seems to feel that the danger is real this time," said Ann.

"The only real danger," Henry said, "is that the war scare can enter a bedroom such as ours and preoccupy two people who love each other."

"That's a rather shallow attitude," she said.

"Politics, war, newspaper headlines, rumors, pronouncements, ideologies are the shallow things," said Henry indignantly. "Events are the toys of old men."

"Please," Ann frowned. If he started quarreling it would end in emotional apologies. She wanted no emotions of any sort.

"Topic discontinued," said Henry. "I've been saving up a story for a rainy day. But since it never rains in Bermuda—"

"A story about what?"

"Elsie," he said.

"Elsie bores me," Ann said.

"That's the point of my story," Henry smiled coaxingly, "her talent as a bore."

"Do you mean Elsie tried to seduce you again?" Ann asked.

"The word 'again' is in error," he said. "*I* was the aggressor in our first maneuvers."

"Really?"

"My God," he thought, "she has no interest in me." He continued to talk. "The night you left the house, Elsie took the offensive."

"I'm sorry her activities bored you," said Ann.

"Nothing happened," said Henry.

"You outwitted her," Ann sneered, and Henry felt like a fisherman alerted by a nibble.

"Outwitting Elsie wasn't too difficult," he said. "A woman has a hell of a time seducing a man who won't co-operate. It's more a matter of physiology than morals."

"I understand," Ann said.

Henry went on, "There's no sense in trying to pull a man into bed who isn't ready to operate. I imagine that feminine reserve is based on this fact, that sex aggression might be a waste of time."

"You don't have to make conversation with me as if I were some data-hungry virgin."

"That's right, you're not," said Henry. "One forgets. It's been so long."

Ann emptied the ash trays near the couch. He watched her with bridegroom concentration. The combination of familiarity and chastity she presented was mysteriously enticing. "A new attitude," he thought, "is like a new body." He wondered what her new attitude was but ended aware only of his own guilt. He decided to make capital out of it, by making his confessions as erotically stimulating as possible.

"Do you care to hear my final Vangie episode?" he asked.

Ann thought, "That idiotic Henry, wheeling out his broken-down cast of Scheherazades."

"I take it you outwitted her, too," she said.

"Ultimately," said Henry. "I gave her to Sam as a political contribution."

"So she told me," Ann said. "I think it's mean."

"To Elsie?"

"No, to Vangie," said Ann. "Sam is quite a comedown after you."

"Thank you."

"I'm really puzzled," Ann said. "I can't understand how you can go to bed with such a creature."

"Bed would have been impossible," he said, "but a couch is different. It's unofficial."

"Poor girl," Ann said, "having to hoist her dresses at a boss's whim."

"A commonplace gesture in our business world," said Henry.

"In all the offices?"

"Most of them," he answered. "A coffee break or a sexual break relieve the monotony of go-getting."

"All those tycoons busy on all those couches," Ann mused, "no wonder the Russians are ahead of us."

He watched her go to the window and look out at the night and sea. "She can't believe in me any more," he thought. "No matter what I am now, I remain the someone else who hurt her."

He said softly, "Please listen."

"I am."

"You're too far away, Ann."

"I can hear very well."

"I wish you would think of my sins as I do," he said.

She seemed not to hear.

"As a page in a closed book," he added.

"I'm not thinking of your sins," Ann said, and turned her face quickly away from him. She was still fearful Henry could see through her forehead and detect its contents. She sighed and thought, "His sins. What an egomaniac." Her heart filled tenderly and painfully with the whisper, "Liza, Liza." She wondered would she ever stop dreaming of her.

"You've kept your schoolgirl delusions about sin," Henry said, "that it's more turbulent than the activities in a legal bed. That's seldom true. I grant you it's more fun flirting with a strange female than with a wife. But when the flirting is over and the bedroom door locked and all the veils are off, the lady of sin seems a bad second to any missus who

249

has kept her shape. Sex with a stranger is usually a super-ficial exercise. Very sketchy, like an improvisation."

Ann smiled. He was wooing her with all the tricks that used to excite her mind and, curiously, her body. They were futile and silly sounding now. But why stop him from talk-ing. It kept her from thinking. And hurting too much.

"Novelty in sex," Henry said, "has a sharp but shallow quality. A new woman offers only her surfaces to caress."

He paused, aware that she wasn't listening. Lying silent, he thought, "I can't make her out. She doesn't hate me or she wouldn't be here. On the other hand, she doesn't love me or she'd be at least vaguely interested in my infidelities. It's amazing how baffling a woman can become by merely keeping silent."

Ann walked to her bed and got into it, Chinese robe and all.

"A good sign," he thought. "She's self-conscious tonight. Last night she peeled down to her nightgown. As if I wasn't there."

The sentence repeated itself—he wasn't there! That was the wrong thing in their honeymoon—he wasn't in the room for her. She had no relation to him, past or present. His wooing bored her. There was something new about Ann. He must look beyond his own guilt.

"Do you mind if I read a while?" she asked.

"Not at all, darling."

He brooded as he watched her profile. She was as far away as a Laplander. He became aware of something in his thought, as if Ann were putting it there. Liza appeared.

Not the chopped-up body in the bloody mess, but a Liza intact and voluptuous. He had avoided talking of her because of the hotel room scene. And he had made no further confessions about Liza. Talking erotically about that horror on the bed would have been humanless. But she wasn't there any longer. His eyes on Ann, an instinct started him, "I'd like to talk about Liza, if you don't mind. I think we ought to talk about her now."

The print blurred under Ann's eyes.

"What about Liza?" she asked quietly.

"I'd like to tell you the truth about her," Henry said. "I said a number of rather emotional things when I was caught—" he elided in time the phrase, "red handed."

Ann thought, "Oh, thank God, he's going to talk about her! Tell me, tell me," she closed her eyes to hide the longing in them.

"I'd like to omit the Liza who died," said Henry, "if you can forget that last horrible look of her."

Ann nodded.

"That horror wasn't Liza," said Henry, "it was Frank Davies. It's unfair to remember her with the mark of his mania on her."

"Remember her as you wish," said Ann, her eyes still closed.

"I will," Henry said, "as a beautiful girl."

"Beautiful, beautiful," Ann's thought echoed.

"I'd like to tell you the truth about her and about me," Henry said, "and if you find it too unpalatable, too much to bear or forgive, well—you can write me off. I can't live with you, even in this hellish Platonic state, without having the truth out."

"I don't think you can hurt me any more," said Ann. He was silent. She thought, "If he would only give her to me. All his memories of her."

"I was in love with her," said Henry. "Not as I was with you. And as I still am. A man has different kinds of love for different women."

"In what way was she different?"

It was the first eager note he had heard in her voice since their arrival. He answered casually, but with a new alertness in him.

"It's a difficult difference to describe to you," he said. "You might not believe or understand it."

"I'll try."

"Because," he looked blandly at the ceiling, "you weren't a woman when you came to me. You're a marriage-made female."

"Like learning to cook for a husband," said Ann. She sounded grim.

Henry continued to the ceiling, "When you fell in love with me, you had a frostbitten libido to offer, full of fuzzy poetry. You were that most American of feminine types—the potential Lesbian. The belligerent virgin full of incipient depravity. I changed you, with a lot of effort. It would have taken a psychoanalyst three years. It took me three months."

"Four," said Ann, "before I earned my diploma."

Henry smiled. He was, he felt sure, on the right train now—Liza.

"You were very sweet," he said, "wanton and uninformed."

"Never mind about me," Ann said, and smiled at him.

"Oh, yes, we were talking about Liza," Henry said, and paused.

"Her difference."

"I don't want to upset you, Ann."

"Oh, please," she tried to sneer, but her voice wavered. She closed her eyes.

Watching her, Henry saw the pulse in her throat quicken its beat. He said meditatively, "Liza was different from the others I've told you about—those paraffined tarts like Vangie. As a matter of fact, the Vangie wenches aren't females. They're female props. Papier-mâché breasts, foam-rubber bellies."

He felt Ann's impatience behind her carefully closed eyes.

"Or they're narcissists," he went on, "who arouse desire in men by swooning over themselves. The lady masturbators with a look like sirens. Who sway their rears when they walk and breathe with their mouths open like "Welcome" door mats.

"My God, he's long winded," thought Ann.

"Liza was none of these phony types," said Henry. "She was the authentic female—a little extra glandular. She was a sort of sexual avalanche."

"Anaconda," Ann said, softly.

Henry was silent. A burn of jealousy went through him. He wondered why, and turned away from the answer.

"You're very good sexually," he smiled at the ceiling, "a

fine lubricity and tender lewdness. Not to mention a beautiful skin and superb shape. Yours is the kind of sexual allure
that can hold a man a lifetime."

"Liza was better," Ann said, and tried to sound mocking.

"Not better," Henry said, "just more concentrated. A sort
of sexual chute-the-chutes. It was like falling into a pit of
sensation."

Ann thought, "She felt nothing for him. What a fool he
was, to be taken in."

She opened her eyes and smiled at him. More, she wanted
more of Liza. He would stop any moment and begin to
psychologize.

"Just what did she do?" she asked boldly. "I mean, it
could have all been in your imagination."

"It wasn't," he said, and the answer he avoided entered
his head. She was in love with Liza. Slowly, with a curious
pain in his heart, he described the sounds, movements and
unsatiety of their dead friend.

"Was she always like that?" Ann asked.

She waited tensely for the answer. To which of them had
Liza lied?

"No, she wasn't," Henry said. "She put on an act at first.
Because she couldn't feel without loving. I saw through her
performance and laughed at it."

"An act?" she pretended bewilderment.

"Phony gyrations with calliope accompaniment," said
Henry. "Then she fell in love with me."

"And the act changed?"

Henry stared at the ceiling.

"I mean, she became different," Ann said softly. She looked at him puffing at his cigar and felt triumphant. He was remembering Liza and seeing the lie of her passion now. Just as she was remembering her and seeing its truth.

"But I must be careful," she thought. "He's sharp. He'll see through me." Then she added, happily, "No, he won't see. No man can see a woman."

They lay silent in their separate beds for several minutes. Ann looked at the Liza he had restored for her. The red bed was gone. Instead of its wrecked occupant, a soft, burning body entered her memory. As she looked at Henry, the image grew brighter, as if a more vivid and detailed Liza were in his mind. Liza was in bed with Henry, preserved in his boastful and erotic memory.

Ann sat up. Henry watched her step out of the bed and take off the Chinese armor, and the bed jacket cuirass . . . With a slow gesture, she shed her nightgown over her head and dropped it to the floor. Henry stared at a white body that seemed like a new language of flesh.

It made no difference now what he thought. Ann looked at her husband as he removed his robe and pajamas. She stood waiting until he lay naked and smiling at her, unlike Henry. Smiling sadly and not moving or holding out his arms in triumph. He was motionless and humble.

She turned off the lights and the room became part of the night. Ann came into the bed beside her husband.

Delight filled her. He hadn't moved. His hands started no male wandering. He lay on his back, waiting—humble and adoring.

Ann whispered, "My darling, my darling."

She leaned over her husband and lowered her mouth to his. Henry thought as he sighed in the dark, "Marriage makes strange bedfellows."

In his first novel in over twenty-five years, Ben Hecht writes of virtuous people who become sinners and sinners who discover that virtue can be very exciting. His story begins when a wife learns that the man she has been married to for eight years is being unfaithful. How can a wife compete with sin? The wildest passion she has to offer only makes her more a wife.

What readers can expect from THE SENSUALISTS is best explained by Mr. Hecht himself in a note to his publisher: "It is in the hope of catching up a modest inch or two with our more amorously erudite forefathers that I have written THE SENSUALISTS. You have only to read Ovid, Rabelais, Aretino, etc., to realize the past was much ahead of us in its sexual insights. My book is a sort of seminar on modern eroticism, such as Ovid might have set down had he been cross-pollinated by Raymond Chandler.

"The trick of the modern novelist is to present the action and dialogue of his bedeviled characters and let the reader figure out their neuroses. The reader becomes a do-